Queen of Hearts

By

Kathryn R. Biel

QUEEN OF HEARTS

Copyright © 2018 by Kathryn R. Biel
Resilient Books

ISBN-13: 978-1-949424-27-0

Cover design by Becky Monson.
Cover image via depositphotos.com by svitlana and welburnstuart.

Dedication

To my "twin" (also soul mate and evil twin, if you believe those Facebook quizzes), Whitney Dineen. I'll always be the Danny DeVito to your Arnold, but I'm just thankful you keep me along for the ride. Oh, and thanks for plotting out this book that time when I was supposed to be helping you.

Chapter 1

My mother always told me not to walk around with my nose buried in a book, otherwise I was likely to fall and kill myself.

I refuse to admit she was right, because I didn't end up dying. Leave it to me to fall not only face first but head-over-heels all at the same time. For someone so obsessed with fairy tales and romance novels, it only seems fitting that I would literally fall out of my shoe and into the waiting arms of the eligible Crown Prince of Montabago.

It's not that I didn't know he was on campus. I mean, the whole world— or at least our little country— knew the prince was there, fulfilling the next step on his journey to becoming king someday. Some of the girls in the cafeteria would keep track of "Stephan Sightings" on a calendar in the employee break room. It's not that I didn't care, but I couldn't waste the energy to care. What would someone like me even say to the prince? He was more handsome in real life than on TV. There's no way he'd ever even look my way.

But when he picked me up he said, "I've been watching you."

I had no reply, first stunned by my trip, and then with the realization of who caught me. My clever reply was something along the lines of "Uhhhh."

The next night, for the first time, I couldn't ignore my awareness of Stephan on campus. Mostly because he was watching me. How hadn't I seen him before? Then I realized something: he was good at standing out when he wanted to and blending in when he needed to.

This went on for weeks before he approached me. "I've been watching you."

"I've noticed." At least I put a few syllables together.

"You work in the cafeteria and in the laundry and when you're not doing that, you're in the library. What are you studying?"

"Nothing." Wow, I was killing it with my conversational skills.

"Why not? This is University, is it not?"

"See aforementioned comment about working in the cafeteria and the laundry. There's no time for something like studying."

"I like to study. Quite a lot. Especially when the subject is as interesting and beautiful as you are."

And if I weren't already falling for—or at least crushing hard on—the prince, that did it. Certainly, I had my doubts that I was little more than a dalliance to him, especially when he said he wanted to keep our relationship a secret.

At first sneaking around was fun. At that point, I understood why our relationship had to be a secret. I knew it wasn't because he was ashamed of me, but rather to avoid the complications that accompanied

6

being a member of the royal family. Evading paparazzi. Making sure we never entered and exited a building together. Scooting off in the middle of the night. I mean, from the first time we met, I wanted to shout from the rooftops that Prince Stephan liked me. Me! Plain old Maryn Medrovovich. I worked in the cafeteria and the laundry for Pete's sake. Yet here Stephan was, having security scurry me into his suite of rooms in the dorm.

Not that I was easy. At least not at first. Not for a long while. The prince's reputation with the ladies was legendary, and I was determined not to be one of *those* women who shamelessly threw themselves at his feet— and other parts of his body. Oh no, I was determined that if Stephan and I were going to be together, it would be because we loved each other. Not because of some inebriated impulse.

However, with each passing day, as Stephan consumed my thoughts, I was relieved that I didn't have to concentrate on my studies. I don't think I could have managed it. All brain power went to Stephan. I thought of his dry wit while I slogged through endless dishes in the cafeteria. I thought of his cunning smile while I cleared tables and emptied garbage bins. I thought of his rock-hard chest (and wondered what else might be rock-hard) while I folded clothes in the steaming laundry.

He didn't seem to care that I was me. I was poor. I was a nobody. I was from a broken home. Every time I brought it up, he held a finger to my mouth, shushing me ever so sweetly. And every time he did that, I wanted to devour him.

Each little thing he did, it seemed, etched him further and further into my heart—and soul. And it wasn't the usual, expected, clichéd things either. It wasn't the roses and chocolates and expensive bottles of wine, even though those were present. It was the small things. The way he'd talk about his dreams for the future—of ruling Montabago—with me at his side. With me he was honest and earnest. He let me see his insecurities. "My father was young when he ascended to the throne. Thirty-five. But he's so much wiser than I. I'm not sure I'll be as good a king as he is. Unless, of course, you're there to keep me straight."

"But Stephan, what would I know about ruling a country or politics or anything? I'm not even educated."

Stephan stretched out, his massive frame filling the bed. "You, my dear, know people and the ways of the world. I know I'll be rubbish without you there."

And in moments like that, he made me feel as if I was queen of the world. It didn't matter to him who my parents were or what jobs I held. All that mattered was me. Being a queen wasn't about riches or luxuries. It was about holding this man's heart in my hands and knowing that he couldn't do it without me. Which is why I not only trusted him with my heart, but with my body as well. After making him wait for almost a year, it was finally time.

The night was much like any other, yet totally different. A sixteen-hour work day for me followed by security sneaking me into Stephan's private suite. Sleep seemed like something frivolous, since all I needed to function was him. Being near him gave me life and energy and sustenance. Tonight was going to be *the night*. I was convinced I meant more to him than a notch on his crown. After all, he's waited a year for me. That's a lot to ask any man.

But when I arrived, it wasn't at all what I expected to find. I was thinking candles, maybe a little Champagne. Some Sade on the stereo. Instead, I found an empty room.

He wasn't even there.

He wasn't even there!

I'd worked sixteen hours straight. I was dog tired and most likely smelled. And he didn't even have the decency to greet me when I arrived? I couldn't believe it. And to think I'd been planning to put out for him. That was it. We were done. I was leaving there and never speaking to that louse again.

But then I saw it. A large box in the middle of the room with my name on it. I pulled open the flaps, wondering if it was possible for Stephan's massive frame to be hiding in there. Nope. All I saw was a stack of wrapped presents. If I had to guess, I would have said they were books. Since Stephan couldn't be bothered to be there to give me instructions, I unwrapped the top one. It was *The Thorn Birds*. Okay. Then I noticed a bookmark. I turned to page five to find the word "I" underlined. I turned the book over, checking to see if it was used, thus explaining the marker and the underline. Putting that aside, I pulled out the next book. *Wuthering Heights*. This book was marked on page one hundred eight-five. The underlined word was "love." The next book—*The English Patient*—had the word "you" underscored on page five.

I started to see a pattern.

The rest of the books—all famous romance novels—revealed the following five words: *Will you please marry me?*

The gasp from my lips was audible as Stephan bursts forth from his hiding place in the bathroom.

"Stephan, what is the meaning of this?"

"My darling, I thought reading was your favorite pastime."

"Reading used to be my favorite pastime. Now it's you."

"My darling, I hope to be like the hero from every romantic story you have ever read. I will dedicate my life to sweeping you off your feet and worshiping the ground you walk on. I live only to serve you and cannot imagine spending one single day without you. Please do me the incredible honor of being my queen. My wife. My love. My best friend."

And with that, he grasped my hand and slid on the most magnificent piece of jewelry I had ever seen. Holy crap. Someday, I was going to be queen!

Chapter 2
Two-ish Years Later

Oh no.

I'm going to pretend this isn't happening. The tightening, the bloating. The urgency. I attempt to ignore my pain as I gaze at the light dancing and refracting off my engagement ring.

The ring weighs down my hand, making it effortful to lift. Not simply because of the size—four point three carats to be exact—but because of the meaning. The symbolism. The sense of responsibility. That responsibility is the direct cause for this current predicament.

It's not as if I didn't know what I was in for when I fell in love with a prince. Actually though, now that I think about it, I had no idea what I was in for. Not really. I was stupid and in love. I didn't know what was to come— how dull and inflexible it would all be. The pomp. The circumstance. The ridiculously long state dinners that were so boring it was all I could do not to doze off. The snippets of things I'd seen on TV didn't truly reflect what it was like to sit there for hours on end with a smile (but not too big a smile) plastered on your face, frozen like a mannequin. The rules. All the rules. So many rules.

Being a newlywed is hard enough. Carrying the weight of a small country into your marriage makes it damn near impossible. Maybe that's why my stomach is in knots.

I look down at the ring again. It means so much. It's been passed down for generations. I think I'm the sixth bride in the Salzach family to have possessed it. There's so much history and so many expectations that go along with this ring. I've been schooled. Endlessly. It means I can't yawn, even though I'm about to fall asleep. It definitely means I can't excuse myself, even though the lobster ravioli isn't sitting well, creating a rather unpleasant churning down below. And it means that I can't tell whatever stuffed shirt windbag who's been pontificating all night to shut up because none of us wants to hear it.

I steal a sideways glance at my husband Stephan, the Crown Prince of the United Republic of Montabago. He looks positively enthralled by the speech. I'll have to ask later why it was so interesting. It's more political stuff I'm sure. The upcoming election. Whether the need for the monarchy still exists, blah, blah, blah.

I take a deep breath and let it out. Probably deeper than I should because I'm fairly confident it comes out like a sigh. At least that's how it's perceived by my father-in-law, King Franklin. I know because he glares at me.

To say he's not my biggest fan would be an understatement. And it's not as if he's subtle about it.

I shift in my seat, pretending my intestines are not starting to scream in protest. There's got to be a natural break in the speeches soon. There'd better be, otherwise I'm going to bring a whole host of shame to the Salzach name.

King Franklin looks at me again. He's watching—waiting—for me to do something—anything—he can use against me. I sit up a bit straighter and focus on breathing deeply. My face sets into its much-practiced expression of benign interest. My hands folded in my lap, my only tell of distress is that I can't stop spinning the massive rock on my left hand. *Spin.* I tilt my head and nod slightly as if agreeing with something Baron Von Windbag up there is saying. *Spin, spin.* A slight furrow to the brow as if he said something that really makes me think. *Spin, spin, spin.* I bite my lip as a roll of pain from my intestines washes over me. I pray that no one can actually hear the rumbling.

I can't take it anymore. Pushing my chair back as delicately as I can, I begin to rise. Stephan turns to me, his eyes ablaze. Oh yes, he's definitely giving me a look. I lean over and whisper, "Please give my regards. I need to leave. Immediately."

Angrily, he whispers, "What can be more important than this?"

I give him a look. He doesn't respond to the plea I'm making with my eyes. "I need to go."

"Go where?" he grumbles through gritted teeth.

"GO," I grumble back as I'm seized by another pain, this one causing me to double over.

I'm sweating and cold all at the same time, but I finally make it out of the stuffy banquet hall. A bored looking sentry points me toward the nearest restroom. I still get lost in this place. It's only been three months, and I'm not even here every day. I forget all my princess training as I lift the skirts of my voluminous gown and sprint down the hall as fast as my Louboutins can carry me. I say a small prayer of thanks that the poofiness of the skirt means I don't have to wrestle my way out of Spanx.

I make it just in time to royally die on the toilet.

I can hear the raised voices. Not shouting; goodness no. When one is a royal, one never raises one's voice beyond a firm tone. It is one of the multitude of rules I had to read, learn, commit to memory, and practice when I agreed to marry Stephan. Actually, I mean when I agreed to marry *Prince* Stephan. My Stephan is a totally different person from the Crown Prince.

Not that I knew it at the time. I only knew I was in love. That kind of all-consuming love that leaves room for neither clarity nor wisdom. Not to say I'm not still in love. I am.

Obviously I am. We're still newlyweds. Newlyweds are always still in love. It's just … well, I love Stephan. I'm not so in love with the royal protocol.

Not even a little.

Which brings me back to my current predicament. I'm hiding out on the throne. And not the literal throne either. I could probably go back out. But staying in here seems preferable to whatever's going on *out there* right now. Because the voice I hear, in addition to Stephan's, is his father's. My father-in-law hasn't had a lot to do with me outside of formal occasions. So, if he's weighing in on my exit from the event, I know I must have broken some sort of royal protocol.

And I'm probably in trouble.

I've managed to stay out of trouble thus far but that's not saying much. I'm sure King Franklin thinks I'm a dimwit or something equally flattering. If I exit the bathroom right now, I will have to say *something* to him. And it's not as if I can tell him the real reason for my swift exodus from the reception.

Heavens, no.

But it's not like I can stay in here all night either, although the powder room couch is surprisingly comfortable. Stephan knocks. "My dear, are you all right in there?"

Time to face the music. "Yes. I'll be out in a moment."

Looking in the mirror, I smooth down the voluminous skirts of my gown. My hair is still perfectly coiffed and my makeup is flawless, as it should be after sitting for hours to have it done. Lately I feel as if I spend more time with Phaedra and Claudine than anyone else. Like they're my only real friends.

No one told me being a princess would be so lonely.

I open the door to see the very concerned face of my husband. He crushes me into a hug. Just as I sink into his warmth, he releases me, remembering that public displays of affection are forbidden. His blue eyes narrow. "My dear, I was worried."

"I'm so sorry, Stephan." My hands cover my lower abdomen. "I wasn't feeling well. I couldn't ... I needed to leave."

He looks down at my hands hovering over my lower belly, where my intestines are still sore. His eyes grow wide. "Really? Already? I didn't think you wanted this so soon. Oh, I'm so—"

I shake my head so rapidly back and forth that a tendril of hair falls down. "No, no, no, that's not it."

"What was the meaning of your rude exit?" King Franklin interrupts, as apparently his royal station gives him right to. Or at least that's what he thinks. "Do you know what kind of impression that will give?"

Stephan places a large hand over mine, flattening both against my abdomen. "We have news."

Oh no. This cannot be happening. He cannot announce my pregnancy. Especially when it doesn't exist. Not knowing what else to do, I stomp my foot down on Stephan's to keep him from telling his father.

While Stephan doubles over, I stand as tall as my 5'1" frame will allow and say, "The news is that I may be developing a bit of lactose intolerance."

The king's face turns dark red. "Ladies do not speak of such things."

"Then perhaps you should not question my motives when you do not want to hear the answers."

I don't know from where that came. Not only is this man my father-in-law and therefore worthy of respect, but he's a king. *My* king. I'll be lucky if he doesn't throw me in the royal dungeon. I'm not sure if there is a royal dungeon, but considering the age of this castle, I wouldn't be surprised if there's a rack around here somewhere. I'm now hoping not to find out the hard way.

I glance over at my husband, whose face is turning an interesting shade of red and purple combined. It'd make a pretty dress. I'll have to try and communicate it to Michele Nowakowski, my personal designer, the next time we talk. King Franklin turns abruptly, stomping off without addressing my rudeness. I feel Stephan's hand grasp my elbow and have no choice but to follow as he virtually drags me down the hall.

Once in the privacy of some room I don't think I've ever been in before, he looks at me, questioning. I can see it all—the hurt, the doubt, the want—written across his face. I tilt my head, waiting for him to begin. I've learned this in the four years I've known him. Stephan has two speeds: jump right in or turtle's pace. The jump right in is rare and only seen in moments where emotion takes over. When he has to formulate and speak, sometimes it can take a while. I know now is one of those moments.

So I wait.

Finally, he's ready. "So, you're not with child?"

I try to understand that Stephan's upbringing was different than mine. Than most people's. His formal speech sometimes amuses me, sometimes annoys me. Currently, it's the latter.

"No, Stephan, I'm not *with child*. Or pregnant. Or knocked up. Or any of those. I had to ... go."

His shoulders sag a bit. "Oh."

He sits down on a settee or lounge or some piece of furniture that I never had in my house growing up.

His 6'3" frame crumples a bit, causing me to rush over and attempt to take him in my arms. It's sort of laughable, especially since there's so much more of him than me. "I'm sorry to disappoint you, honey."

Stephan won't look at me. "No, it's my fault. I know you said you didn't want to start trying yet, but, well, I was hoping something would happen."

This makes my spine stiffen. "I'd like to think that you mean well with that comment, but a baby is not something you just hope *happens*."

"Don't you want to have a baby with me? You said you did. We've discussed this." His tone is more annoyed than I've ever heard it. "Multiple times."

"And I do. Someday. Not today. It's too soon. I'm … this … we're … still too new."

"We've been together for four years, Maryn. How much time do you need? Do you doubt my love for you?" Now he looks up at me and I see the pleading in his eyes. He pulls me tight to him, as if he's afraid to let go.

I slowly let out the breath I didn't know I'd been holding. I can't believe I have to explain this to him. It annoys me that he doesn't know it without me spelling it out. "Steph and Mar have been together for four years. Prince Stephan and Princess Maryn are still very new. And I'm still getting used to it. Finding my way. Figuring out where I fit in and what to do next. Let's face it, you're figuring this out too. You're not the same as when you were at University either. It's not easy like it was then. It's no longer simple. I don't want to add a baby to that mix until things are a little more settled. I'm not saying I never want one. I'm saying not right now."

He nods. "I understand. But you must as well. It is very important that we have an heir."

This. This is what I'm struggling with, but I don't know how to tell him, as I don't know how to tell him most things these days. I want our baby with his piercing blue eyes and red hair and my defined cheekbones. I want a living expression of our love. Because that and an heir are two different things.

And I have no interest in producing an heir.

Chapter 3

The bed depresses as Stephan's large body rolls out, while I lay still, eyes closed but mind racing. A chill seeps into the void and I huddle down under the down comforter a bit longer. Perhaps I doze for a minute or two, because the next thing I know Stephan is showered and dressed in black slacks and a cobalt shirt that makes his eyes positively glow.

I peek out at him.

He's stunning. More stunning than the first time I saw him outside the library. Of course, I didn't see him so much as fall into him. Stupid cracked sidewalk. But as I went pitching forward, falling right out of my shoe, I landed in a pair of large, strong arms that greeted me with a low chuckle.

It took me a minute to place him as he basically picked me up and put my feet back underneath me. I didn't even care that I had one bare foot. His size took my breath away. His eyes, dancing with amusement at my clumsiness, made me weak in the knees. Only after staring into them for a moment, wishing it was forever, did I realize who my knight in shining armor was. How fitting. I wanted to be irate because I'm not the type to trip and fall, but there, in his arms, I could have kissed that crack in the sidewalk.

I don't often see that amusement in his eyes these days. Certainly not this morning. I know he's hurt that I don't want to have a baby just yet. Babies make things harder. And this is already hard enough.

I know he doesn't—can't—see that. He doesn't know how. He only knows what he's been bred to know. As do I. And I know having a child at the wrong time can end the marriage.

Like it did for my parents.

In all honesty, my dad probably had one foot (or other body part) out the door before my mother's surprise announcement, but that was all it took for him to rebel in the worst possible way.

With the next-door neighbor.

I am still mortified every time I think about it, despite the fifteen years that have elapsed since.

And the source of my embarrassment is part of the reason King Franklin hates me. My common, soiled past. It's not as if I can help where I was born or what my parents did. And it's not like the royals are without scandals themselves ... they're just *royal* scandals, which makes them more acceptable. I don't think my father-in-law will ever get over the fact that his son married a commoner. So it doesn't matter if I master royal protocol or not. I won't be enough for him.

At least I'm enough for his son. I hope.

"What's on the agenda for today?" I call to Stephan as I finally rise from my comfy cocoon of bedding. He's at the door, his hand on the ornate knob. He doesn't face me while talking, which speaks volumes in and of itself.

"Valentia will bring you your schedule as she has every day."

I try to ignore the curtness in his voice. "I see. Thank you. Have a good day." I'm using my princess voice. The one that has been carefully crafted through diction and vocal lessons.

Once he leaves, I sit on the edge of the bed, willing the tears not to come. I work on my facial composure, my body language. How to regally handle such an ego crushing moment without crumpling.

Princesses don't crumple.

Nor do they cry. Or raise their voice. Or not want to bear an heir.

Princesses belong to the people and put their own needs aside for the good of the country.

That's why I agreed to the ludicrous idea of going on a reality TV show to have my clothes made in the first place. I was told that I needed to do this for the monarchy. I would have much preferred to pick out a designer in the privacy (said, priv-acy, of course) of my own home. I'm not going to lie; I love having a personal designer. It's perhaps one of the best—perhaps only—perks, of this gig as of yet.

Plus, the royal handlers thought it would be a good way to train me to be on camera. I don't know how they got King Franklin to agree to it, the old stuffed shirt that he is, but somehow he consented. I'm sure it had to do with gaining votes in the election.

I absolutely hate watching footage of *Made for Me*. I look like a stuck-up prig on that show. Michele, the winning designer, was about the only genuine person there. I can attest that she is exactly the same in real life as she was on camera. I wish I could say the same for me.

But I knew, or thought I knew, what I was signing on for when I agreed to marry Stephan. I've read all the fairy tales and romance novels. I thought I knew how it would be once we had the big, climactic wedding. Even if I had known better, I'm not sure it would have made a difference. By then, it was too late, really. I would have promised the Devil my soul to be with him.

We were engaged—or at least had promised ourselves to each other—a year before any official announcement was made. Those first two years of our relationship were something special and magical that we'll never have again. It really was the storybook romance. Because it was just us, practically hidden away at the university, protected from the outside world and the palace. He was so handsome and gregarious, his posture impeccable after those five years of military service. The strength in his arms, his back. His chiseled features and dancing blue eyes.

He made me feel as if I was the only person on the planet. Like a princess.

But today, like almost every day since we've been married, and many before it, the needs of the country come first.

I knew that when I signed on. I know that now. It's hard though.

I thought this was supposed to be easy. Meeting Prince Charming certainly was. I'm a Cinderella story if I've ever heard one, right down to the shoe. So why aren't we blissfully happy right now?

Partially, because I'm bored. My days are either jam packed with boring public appearances and royal things or they're empty, much like today appears to be since Valentia has yet to make her appearance. Stephan's off doing his princely thing, whatever that is. He tells me he has frequent meetings. And I'm alone. Sure, I'm catching up on my reading, but there are only so many books, even for me. I never thought I'd say that. Books used to consume all my free time, not that there ever was much of it. If I wasn't working in the laundry or the cafeteria or helping Ma out around the house and with Tomas, I was reading. I never seemed to have enough time for it. Now it's, well, kind of boring. I'm sick of the sticky sweet "and they all lived happily ever afters." Probably because my ever after is not turning out that way. I need to find something else to fill my day. I've brought up this issue with Stephan, but it seems to have fallen on deaf ears. I'm sick of being sent to events that have no meaning for me or doing nothing. I need to do something that matters.

In the meantime, I'm considering taking up a hobby, but I don't know what I would be allowed to do as a palace dweller. I'm not in the mood to learn to play the harpsichord. I don't even know if that's really still a thing, but in all the books, that's what the women do. Sure, they're set in Regency England, but stuck in this castle, I don't feel as if much has changed. I used to knit when I was young, but I'm sure that's much too commonplace for the royal palace.

Those class divisions don't seem like history most days.

Once through the shower and dressed in respectable slacks and twin sweater set, complete with pearls, I wait for Valentia to bring me my schedule. I don't know where she is today. Obviously no one needs me and I've nothing to do. This doesn't help the mood I'm in. I hate everything. I hate my current book. I hate this outfit. It's not a Michele original, that's for sure. It's something some other staff member bought for me to augment my wardrobe. I understand the need to look respectable, but this is ridiculous. Just because I met Stephan in front of the library doesn't mean I need to look like a librarian my whole life. No offense to librarians, because book people are awesome people, and if I had to pick a career, I probably would be a librarian. But still, this will not do.

Texting Michele, I ask her when she's coming to visit again. As part of winning the show, she is at my beck and call for the next year and will make anything I need her to make. I know the producers and the royal people thought her services would be primarily for public appearances, but I don't want to be caught dead looking how I look. God forbid Stephan see me like this. He'll never be turned on by me again, since I don't think he has a librarian fetish.

I guess that would solve the heir problem.

Texting back and forth is irritating me so I turn to the old standby, video chatting. "Michele, look at me. This is what they pick for me to wear. I look ... I look ... " I can't find the right words.

"Boring and dull and old." Michele's right on target, so I can't even be offended. "Bring me over to your closet and show me what's in there so we can do better."

I walk across the room to the massive walk-in closet that's bigger than the living room of my mother's house. The clothes are sectioned off by type. Gowns, dresses, skirts, blouses, sweaters, pants. For anyone in the fashion world, it's to-die-for orgasmic. I think it's okay. Now if it were a library, that would be another story.

After panning around so much that I'm a bit dizzy, Michele has picked out a hunter-green blouse with sheer sleeves and a conservative neckline. She thinks it'll work with my current pants, so I quickly put the phone down and change for her to see. Well, I'll be. She's a magician.

"All you need to do is add a belt and a long necklace, preferably one with a sizeable pendant. That green is perfect for you."

"Even though it's August? Shouldn't I wait until autumn to wear this color?" I turn and look at myself in the mirror. It is a good color, set off by my dark hair. It makes my eyes look greener than normal. "You know what, I think green should be my color. I like what it's doing for my eyes."

Michele agrees. "I'll make a note of that in your file. I love how you look in blue, but the green has a great effect as well. Your next special occasion dress will be green. Speaking of which, do you have any idea of what you'll need next?"

I shake my head. "No, you'll have to get your people to talk to Valentia and her people."

Michele lets out a little giggle. I can see her hand fly to her mouth, trying to cover it up. I bet that came off as super stuck-up and she's laughing at how ridiculous I sound.

"What? I sound snooty, don't I? I'm sorry. I don't mean to. I'm not snooty by nature. I—"

Michele is frantically waving her hand. "Oh, no, Maryn. It's not that. It's that I have *people*. I can't even. Like literally. I can't even believe that I have people."

I find Michele quite amusing. She's a bit flighty but has more talent in her pinky finger than most have in their entire bodies. We're about the same height, which gave her a distinct edge when designing clothes for me.

Plus, the wedding gown she designed for me ... pure heaven.

"You deserve to have people. You are wonderfully talented. I'm so lucky to have you working for me for this year. I should have you make me tons of things so I'm all set for after our contract expires." I'm more thinking out loud at this point. I'm not even sure I'm allowed to do that.

"Oh, my God, really? You can't be serious? Oh my God. I can't even." The shaking of the video on the phone is making me dizzy. Remind me not to make Michele too excited when video chatting again.

"I'll check with my ... people ... but I'm sure we can work something out." I don't know if we can. I'm not sure how any of this works. To this point, since going public, I've been told what to do. I haven't asked for anything. That should count for something, right? I've been low maintenance as far as princesses go.

Finally satisfied with how I look and no longer channeling my inner librarian, I'm ready to leave my suite and face the day. Valentia never showed up with a schedule, so I'm on my own to figure out how to entertain myself.

It's after eleven, which means lunch can't be far off. I didn't eat breakfast, only partaking of the tea that had been sent to my room. When I was a child, I'd dreamed of the day when I could be an adult and drink coffee like my dad. Now I don't want anything associated with him, which leaves me depending on tea as my primary source of caffeine. Tea is boring, much as I'm becoming. I miss coffee.

Just another reason to hate my father, though I surely don't need one.

But since the intestinal distress last night, I'd been a little hesitant to put anything more in my stomach first thing in the morning. Now it's screaming in protest. Only taking three wrong turns, I finally find the large industrial kitchen. The staff stops and looks when I walk in, barely a pot clattering to fill the sudden silence. I know I toured here when I first moved in but since then my meals have either been sent to my room or were part of large, formal events. I have to admit I've been enjoying the fact that I don't have to cook and plan meals anymore, but I sort of miss that normalcy too. Even in the year of the engagement, I was sheltered in an apartment with full staff that came and went like my own personal magical fairies who did everything for me. I wish we could still live there instead of in the palace.

"May we help you, Your Highness?"

I pause for a moment before I speak, the rule about never using fillers such as um and ah rearing its ugly head. "My agenda was a bit light today, so I dallied about more than I should have this morning. I seemed to have forgotten to eat breakfast. I was wondering if I can make myself a bite to eat?"

A buxom middle-aged woman lumbers forward, causing me to retreat toward the door. This must be the Frau Einshuchtern I've heard so much about. Phaedra and Claudine, my royal hair and makeup team, are absolutely terrified of her. "No, I'm afraid we cannot do that Your Highness," she answers in no uncertain terms. She's probably almost six feet tall, with a build not dissimilar to that of a linebacker. She makes me want to hide in a corner and suck my thumb. Or wet my pants. Or both. This is undoubtedly her kitchen and I have undoubtedly overstepped my bounds by asking for a meal outside of the scheduled time.

I would rather starve than cross this woman.

"Um, okay." Crap. I'm supposed to say neither um nor okay. I hope no one tells Valentia or the diction coaches. "Thank you anyway." There are plenty of people throughout the world who don't get three squares a day. I'll survive. I turn back to exit the way I entered just as my stomach lets out a large gurgle, as if emphasizing my plight.

"Your Highness, no. Stop." The cook's voice is so commanding that it roots me to my spot. I'm a bit afraid to turn around and face her. Slowly I work up the courage, trying to make my petite frame seem as large as possible, not that it can compare to hers. Sometimes, I really hate being short.

"Lunch will be served in fifteen minutes. I was not informed that you'd be joining His Highness and His Royal Highness but I'll have Magda set a place right now. Please excuse this oversight."

I don't know what to say. I obviously was not included in this luncheon. Frau Einshuchtern knows that as well as I do. My eyebrow lifts. She gives a curt nod as I follow her into the dining room.

All eyes turn in my direction. The feeling of wanting to wet my pants is back. I know I'm hungry and all but what did I just get myself into?

Chapter 4

Other than sheer panic, I don't know what exactly to feel because there are all sorts of emotions swirling. In addition to hunger, irritation—no, anger—is competing for the top spot. I think it just won.

There are my husband and father-in-law and four other dignitaries, including Baron Von Windbag from last night, all having lunch together. Or they're about to, from the looks of the salad plates being handed out.

In addition to the hunger and anger, which have combined into an overpowering hanger, there's a distinct sense of mortification. *Why was I excluded from this gathering?* Especially since nothing else was on the agenda, obviously.

The staff, led by Magda, has quickly created a place for me across from Stephan. Good. I plan on glaring at him for the duration of the meal. Trying to save face, I straighten up and tilt my head slightly upward. "I do apologize for my tardiness. I didn't realize how late I was and then, well, frankly I got lost again. I'm afraid I'm no good without an escort."

Baron von Windbag—I think his real name is Baron von Windringham, but Windbag suits him so much better—clears his throat. "Think nothing of it, Your Highness. Prince Stephan said you were still under the weather from last night and that you didn't feel up to joining us."

So Stephan excluded me from this. Why would he do that? If this is all because of the heir crap, he can shove it. "Yes, well, I am sorry for my swift exit. As my husband indicated, I was rather unwell. But I'm much better today and anxious to be out of my suite."

Someone else at the table—I know I should know who he is but I simply can't keep them all straight—interjects. "Princess Maryn, so lovely to see you again."

Oh fiddlesticks. That means I should really know who he is.

"Now, Daniel, do you really think it's fair to expect my wife to remember everyone she met on our wedding day? I mean, she was marrying me. I doubt she could focus on anything else."

Everyone at the table, with the exception of King Franklin, lets out a polite laugh. And in this moment, my irritation at his previous slight forgotten, I remember why I fell so absolutely, stupidly, head-over-heels in love with Stephan. That cocky sense of humor. The fact that he knew I didn't know the man's name and swooped in to save me. I feel my anger melting away. A smile betrays the last holdout of righteous indignation.

Until they start talking again, totally leaving me out of any conversation. It's not as if I have much—anything really—to contribute, but still. Rude. They are again debating the upcoming election. It's still four months off, and it dominates all topics all the time. Even at our wedding, which was perhaps one of the most dull affairs I've ever attended. Yes, I know it's a big deal that the public will decide whether or not the monarchy should continue as the ruling power of Montabago. If they—we—lose, the titles will remain but actual governmental power will shift to an elected body. The royal family will be relegated to serving as figureheads. Not that I'm allowed to say it in the presence of, well, anyone, but I don't know that it would be the end of the world if it happened. Sometimes monarchies tend to be out of date and out of touch with the people.

I'm not really paying attention, as the talk of points and numbers and approval ratings is a bit over my head, when I realize I've been specifically addressed. "I'm sorry, Daniel. I didn't catch that last bit."

He smiles. "I asked, Your Highness, what it is you'd be doing if not slumming here?" Stephan laughs and elbows his buddy, and I notice King Franklin and Baron von Windbag exchange uncomfortable glances.

And then the reason for my exclusion at this intimate luncheon becomes crystal clear. The king wants to hide me as much as possible lest the public know what my background truly is; not that the press didn't do a thorough and smashing job of dredging up quite a bit. I play with my fork while considering my answer. "That's hard to say. I did quite a bit of this and that until I met Stephan."

"I thought you two met at the university?" Daniel looks perplexed.

"Technically we did, although I was not enrolled at the time." I see my father-in-law's face start to darken. "I'm afraid by that time I'd dropped out and was working to make ends meet, so I was working at the university. Or for the university, I should say. You see, my father left and my brother is disabled, and the burden of his care fell on my mother and me. I had very much wanted to continue taking classes, but eventually that expenditure became frivolous."

Baron von Windbag clears his throat, announcing his intent to speak. Oh joy. "I find that a common misconception amongst certain groups of *people*—" His pointed look at me tells me what kind of *people* he's talking about, "is that education is an unnecessary expense. Perhaps one does not always realize that investment in bettering oneself is always a worthwhile expenditure."

And this is why I'm starting to side with the Republicists, and why they stand a very good chance of winning the election. I put my fork down and place my napkin gently on the table. Pushing my chair back, I look the baron in the eyes. "When one is forced to choose between a roof over one's family's head and food on the table and a philosophy textbook, one's choice is rather clear and obvious."

King Franklin's already stalwart posture stiffens. If he were any more erect, he'd be made of titanium.

Daniel laughs, his jovial tone cutting through the tension. "Cripes, Steph, no wonder you're keeping her out of the spotlight except for the ridiculousness with that television show. If you let her speak, the people will definitely think she's anti-mon."

"Of course she's not anti-mon. She's my wife. She'll be the mother to the next heir to the throne. Maryn will be integral in continuing the monarchy for the next hundred years."

Finally, King Franklin breaks his silence. "Yes, this is why we had to go to such lengths to legitimize a commoner. We cannot allow one iota of leverage for the Republicists to challenge our right to rule."

"Yes, there was quite the vetting process in being allowed to marry Prince Stephan. In addition to a thorough genealogy search, as well as humiliating physical to see if I would be able to produce a royal offspring, there was the tedious years spent at the Princess Academy learning how to be a proper princess."

Daniel and Stephan laugh. The king and baron are not so amused. The other two gentlemen at the table look rather uncomfortable. Good. My work here is done.

"Princess Academy? I didn't know such a thing existed." Daniel sits back and takes a sip of his wine. "Do tell me all about it."

"Well, I'd been hoping my invitation would arrive by owl, but it was sent on a glass slipper instead. Those things leave terrible blisters and they're not the least bit practical for standing all day."

Stephan gives me a warm smile. "See? See why I had to defy order and tradition and make this incredible woman my wife?"

Since it's not as if the king can publicly object to me, he is forced to concede. "Yes, well, compared to some of the gold diggers you have associated with in the past, we were at least sure Maryn's intentions were in the right place."

I think that's about as nice a compliment as I've ever received—or probably will ever receive—from my father-in-law. Unable to help myself, I give him a small smile.

With that, unable to find anything else pleasant to say, he stands to leave. As per protocol, we stand and watch him exit, followed closely by Baron von Windbag. I think, technically, Stephan and I should have exited the room following the king, but I don't stand much on ceremony. The other two dignitaries file out after Stephan gives them a nod, leaving us and Daniel.

"Finally the old folks are gone. Let's go find a comfortable place to chat." Daniel claps Stephan on the back and offers me his arm. I take it gently, not sure of what else to do, and we wander out to find a sitting room. I'm actually familiar with the room we choose and am finally able to be at ease.

Once we're settled, Daniel casually leans back, crossing ankle over knee. "So, tell me more about yourself, Your Highness. I have a feeling there's so much more to you than the tiny drivels of information the palace has let out."

I'm not sure what to say or how much to say. This type of situation has been strictly coached in princess class. Hating that I need to do it, I seek out Stephan for guidance. He smiles and nods, but somehow I don't yet feel comfortable.

"Go ahead, darling. Daniel is here to help. Plus, I've known him since my secondary days."

"Well, I'm not sure my story is that special. In fact, I know it's not. I grew up in a lower-middle class family, in a lower-middle class town, doing lower-middle class things. My parents' relationship was not fantastic, so out of desperation, my mother did what women trapped so often do and had a baby to save her marriage. This is when I was fourteen. My brother was born with Down syndrome, and that was all my father needed to totally disregard any semblance of adherence to his marriage vows. When I was sixteen, he ran off with the next-door neighbor. My mother had to take care of my brother, so I cut my classes back to part time and finally dropped out of school altogether to work to provide what money the Support couldn't."

This has Daniel's attention. He's leaning forward, practically salivating at the gossip. "So you didn't complete Secondary?"

"No, I did. But after that, I tried the Uni, but well, I found employment and food was a better option."

"And what of your brother and mother now?"

"My brother will always need round-the-clock supervision. He's in a program during the day and with Ma at night. Their living accommodations and support are much better now, thanks to Stephan. There are plans for a group home when he turns eighteen next year."

Daniel claps his knee. "Jesus, Steph, you're sitting on a gold mine here. This—*this*—is what we need to be telling the people about. I can't believe your father doesn't want her out in the public spotlight more."

I start to shake my head vehemently. I've been warned never to speak of this. Mentions of such distasteful things would certainly be detrimental to the cause of the monarchy.

Stephan takes my hand, obviously picking up on my distress. "Do you really think so, Daniel?"

"Of course. It's a bloody gold mine. The Republicists's main argument is that the monarchy is out of touch with the common man. What is a better way to show that they aren't than this?"

Stephan nods. "You're right. It might be good to really show from where Maryn came and what she has endured to get here."

"Wait a blasted minute. This story is mine, and I don't know that I want it plastered all over the news. I wouldn't mind being out there, helping with literacy or scholarships for underprivileged children, but I'm not sure I'm comfortable exploiting the story of my brother. And for what? And why do you have a say anyway?"

Stephan turns to me. "It's all right darling. Daniel has been appointed as a public relations specialist."

"By whom? How is he qualified?" I'm hoping he's a hack and I can get him off this trail. I don't want them digging around my past. Stephan knows it and that's enough. I don't need the whole world to see my shame and embarrassment. It was bad enough when we were first announced a year ago, but the palace kept a tight lid on some of the more salacious details. And now, to keep bringing it up over and over. To know that I come from nothing. To know that my father treated us with such disrespect, obviously because we were not worthy of respect. And how his actions not only broke my mother's heart, but mine as well, costing me my first love. What I did made me no better than my father, and *that* is what I don't want the whole world knowing, even for the benefit of an election. Especially not for the benefit of the election.

"Not only has it been my job for the past several years, but I have an in with the king's most trusted advisor."

"Baron von Windbag? He listens to something else besides his own pontification?"

Stephan's face turns bright red at my remark. Daniel offers up an amused smile. "Well, I would hope so, considering the—what did you call him?—windbag—is my father."

Chapter 5

This is why I'm not allowed to speak to the public or do anything other than sit there and look pretty. Not that I'm qualified to do much else, and frankly, if it weren't for my support team, I wouldn't even be qualified to look pretty.

How does one even rebound from that?

Daniel laughs. "Oh, that's a good one. I can't believe I've never heard it before. Yes, my father can be quite the pompous ass. And that's why Steph has insisted I come in to work on the campaign. To keep it civilized and dignified but to make sure we win."

"So we don't become a world-wide laughing stock and embarrassment, like what's going on in America," Stephan agrees.

"Oh, thank goodness. Their election is still three months off and it seems as if it's dominating the world news. And not for good reasons either. No, I don't want to be associated with anything like that. And you know I'm willing to help. I'm just not that comfortable with the details of my personal life being aired out. There are some things I'm not terribly proud of. Of which I'm not terribly proud," I quickly correct.

Daniel smiles. "Oh do tell. Steph has his own closet of skeletons. We can air them out."

"I doubt my husband has many skeletons or has done things of which he is ashamed." I give myself a mental high five for remembering the correct grammar, even though it probably doesn't matter in this moment.

"Oh, Steph, have you not told this poor woman of your time in Secondary? Or when you got out of the army? Or when—"

"Enough Daniel. Maryn knows enough. She knows that I had my fun and sowed my wild oats and all that ended the day I met her. I was instantly besotted and will stay that way until the day I die."

He's right. Since the night we met, he's never glanced at another woman. I can't help but smile at my husband. My love. "Then perhaps the story we want to tell the public is how you made a fool of yourself chasing me all around the Uni as I went from job to job and got me fired from the kitchen staff because you kept creating such a disturbance with your presence."

"I got you your job back," Stephan puffs indignantly.

"No, you think you got me my job back. I actually promised my supervisor that I would give her a pair of your boxers in exchange for resuming my employment." I wink at Daniel. "It's a good thing I worked in the laundry as well."

"The kitchen *and* the laundry? You're a real-life Cinderella! That's the angle we have to take."

"Except I've no wicked stepmother or stepsisters. Just a wonderful, equally hardworking mother and the most pleasant developmentally disabled brother who is an absolute delight to know."

"Well, Steph, Princess, I think I've got a bit to start with. I may head to your hometown and check things out, but I think the next news coming from the palace will sound a lot like a fairy tale."

I'd thought the mudslinging and muckraking going on in America was terrible. Part of me lived in fear that Daniel would uncover the *thing* that had thus far remained a deep-buried secret. The entire world knew my father was a deadbeat and that Tomas was disabled. But there was that one thing they'd yet to discover. This fear was winding me up. A day went by. Then two. Then a month. Surely someone would talk. George's father still lived in that house next to my old one. I don't know where George is. If he's even still at home. I hope Daniel doesn't find him. Deep hurts don't stay buried.

Stephan didn't understand my concern as the days passed, and I continued to struggle with a nagging anxiety. I'd tried to tell him what happened, and what I'd done, but he didn't think it was a big deal. "Kids' stuff really. No one will think twice. It's not as if my handlers didn't know I was a bit of a wild child for a bit. I wasn't too bad though. Not really. Or at least nothing that couldn't be taken care of."

"What do you mean by that?"

"Well, you know. The usual. Girls mostly."

"Girls? How many girls are we talking?" We've never really delved this deeply. I didn't want to know. I still don't, but I can't refrain from asking.

Stephan looks at me in the mirror as I'm standing behind him. He's slowly unbuttoning his shirt, undressing for the night. "Honestly, I don't know. It's not as if it matters. The only thing that matters is that you are the only woman I will ever be with again."

I let those words soothe me as Stephan turns to embrace me. "I cannot remember another face—another voice—another body—when I am with you."

His words make me stiffen for a moment because as he says that, George's image springs to mind. His green eyes, so hopeful, then crushed by my words. My actions. If Stephan knew how cruel and heartless I could be, he might not feel the same about me.

I push those thoughts out of my mind and force myself to be here, present, with my husband. With his muscular frame, gorgeous buttocks, and sinful mouth. Ahhh, yes. Conjugal bliss.

Until, that bliss—well, just about a moment before the actual bliss—is so rudely interrupted by a banging on the door. Not just a banging, but a loud, incessant banging. Unrelenting. Damn, my bliss is going to have to wait.

Stephan hauls himself off the bed and angrily wraps a blanket around his lower half. Oh good. I can still ogle his strong back and chest while he commences to rip whoever interrupted us a new one. Stephan gives a brief glance back to make sure I've covered up before yanking open the door.

"This had better be damn important. The world better be on fire or something."

Daniel bursts in. "Oh, it is important, but I'd not consider it good news at all." Daniel glances in my direction and nods curtly. "Princess." Then he looks back at Stephan and then back at me. "Um, Your Highness, perhaps you could excuse Steph and me for a moment."

"Whatever you have to say to me, you can say in front of my wife."

Daniel looks between Stephan and me. I'm sort of wishing I were dressed in more than a sheet, as I have a feeling this is bad.

"This is bad."

"Can we get dressed? I'd feel more ready to handle this news if .... perhaps ... if I were less exposed." Daniel nods and quickly exits the room. Our dressing is hasty, fueled by anticipation of this news that will surely change our lives. We adjourn to the office that's part of our bedroom suite. No one besides housekeeping staff is allowed in our bedroom, which indicates how serious Daniel must feel this matter is. The pit in my stomach, a small annoyance over the past month, grows wide and tugs.

We sit staring at each other. Unable to take it a moment more I ask, "Would you like me to call for tea or coffee? I'll have a service sent up."

Daniel shakes his head. "This is not a tea or coffee occasion. Whiskey maybe." He settles his gaze on Stephan. "It's bad, mate. Really bad."

Stephan swallows hard and nods for him to continue.

"Dominicka Nochten."

I have no idea what he's talking about. It's not about George, so I don't care what it is about. It's not about my atrocious behavior with the kindest soul in the world.

"I don't know who that is," Stephan answers.

"Obviously, since the name means nothing to either of us, it can't affect us that much then can it?" I smile hopefully, but the wan look on Daniel's face tells me different.

"Steph, I believe you met Dominicka Nochten during your first year out of Secondary. In that time before you started your military service."

Stephan laughs. "Hard to recall. I met a lot of people back then."

"Unfortunately you did, you bloody wanker. She's got a kid."

Stephan shrugs again. "Well, she didn't tell me that when I met her."

Daniel stands up. "No, you fool. She has one now. He's fourteen."

I see Stephan's eyes darting back and forth, trying to process. To figure it out. I do the same. He joined the army when he turned twenty. Stephan is thirty-four now. Oh no.

"Well, certainly, it's a possibility, but I'm sure a lot of women have tried—and failed—to claim such a thing in the past. It's a job hazard."

"No, it's a hazard of not being able to keep it in your pants."

Stephan shrugs. "It's all in the past. I've sown my wild oats and am now happily settled down with my love." He reaches over and takes my hand. It's a bit awkward considering we're sitting about three feet apart on matching King Louis chairs, but I understand his need to make the gesture.

Daniel hands Stephan a picture and the color drains from his face.

"What? What is it?"

Stephan wordless hands the picture to me. I might as well be looking at a photograph of Stephan. A blood test to determine paternity will not be necessary. I hand the picture back. I've seen enough.

"But ... I .... why is she coming forward now?"

With this, Daniel drops his head into his hands.

"C'mon, Daniel. Tell me. It's the election bringing her out of the woodwork, right?"

Without revealing his face, Daniel nods. "She's demanding a large sum of money to stay silent."

"How large?"

"No way in hell."

Stephan and I answer at the same time. My husband turns to look at me. "No way in hell?"

"Did I stutter? No way in hell. If that boy is your son, which it's pretty obvious to anyone with eyes that he is, then so be it. What's done is done. That stallion left the barn fourteen years ago."

"This will be disastrous for the monarchy," Stephan tells me. Daniel nods in agreement.

"Things happen. Especially with foolish young men who think they're all that and a bag of chips. It's not as if this is the first time a member of a royal family will have procreated out of wedlock." History is full of children born outside the confines of marriage. Surely both Stephan and Daniel know this.

Daniel is on his feet and pacing. "It's not that simple. Perhaps we could have withstood this but the timing—it could not be worse."

"Then you use it to your advantage." I don't understand how they can't see the positive side, as they both stare blankly at me. "If this woman chooses to step forward, then you welcome her—and the child—with open arms. Show that the monarchy is not out of touch with its citizens. The public cannot blame you if you knew nothing about this child until now. If anything, you're the victim, having been denied a chance to know your son all this time."

Stephan jumps up. "That's right. I am the victim here. The child and myself. We've been denied so much. I would have visited him over the years. Maybe taken in a football match or something."

It's about at this point when my blood starts to run a bit cold. There are words in my head—so many words—but I can't yet express them. For once I do, I have a feeling life as I know it will change.

And I don't think for the better.

Chapter 6

"And then he said ..." I break off, unable to continue with the horrible thing.

Michele looks up from her sketchbook. "You can't leave it like that. What did he say?"

I hadn't really needed Michele to visit based on fashion needs, but after the chaos of the last few weeks, I realized I was lacking a friend. "He said, 'It's not as if it matters. The boy will never be heir to the throne.'"

"What? No. Why not?"

"Because he's illegitimate."

Michele's brow wrinkles even though she's resumed drawing. I assume it's in disapproval of my news, but with her you never know. It could be because her design isn't working. "So what about the kid then? Does he know about his father?"

"I don't know. The mother is coming here tomorrow for a meeting so we can discuss how this will be handled." Which, of course, was a load of bunk. The king and his lackeys already knew exactly what they were going to say and do. I had a feeling it would involve throwing boatloads of money at her to make her disappear, which I tell Michele in a hushed voice lest any of the staff overhear me. It's not as if the mother is an innocent bystander. A gold digger is more like it, but I know she'll get her payday.

"Can they do that?"

"This is the ruling governmental body. It's not North Korea or anything like that, but I have a feeling the outcome will be exactly what King Franklin wants it to be."

"Is that okay with Stephan and you?"

This has been a very touchy subject between us since the morning Daniel dropped the bombshell. "Stephan's ... well ... it's not bothering him. At all. He's taking the attitude that he didn't know so there's nothing to be done about it. He's not opposed to spending some occasional time with the lad." That was a direct quote. I sort of hated Stephan the moment he said it. The hate was fleeting, but I couldn't believe that was his attitude. He was like a stranger standing there before me.

"How would he feel if it were your child?"

"That's the worst part." It was, truly. I'm not sure if I can even admit it to Michele.

"I don't know that it can get much worse." She turns her sketchbook toward me, showing a great dress and evening gown. "I'll do the day outfit next. Pants?"

"Yes, pants." I take a deep breath. "The worst part is that Stephan is still all gung-ho to have a baby. To produce a *legitimate* heir."

"But he's got a kid."

"Let's just say the word 'bastard' has been batted about a bit more than I'm comfortable hearing."

Michele drops her pencil. "Isn't this the twenty-first century?"

I nod. "I thought so. But it appears we're stuck in the eighteenth century here."

"If that's the case, I'm designing all the wrong looks. This skirt clearly shows your ankles, and I'll need to add a corset and a bustle."

"Spanx are bad enough. If you add a corset or anything—other than shoes—that has laces, I'm out," I laugh.

"So, what are you going to do then?"

"I've no love lost for Dominicka—that's the mother, but I can put that aside for the sake of the child. I think it's terrible that he's had to grow up all this time without his father. Can you imagine what he thinks? How that makes him feel?"

Michele shakes her head. "I can't; not really. But you remember Kira? Her dad left when she was a teenager, and now her husband has walked out on her too. She's got huge issues because of it. My cousin Tony's been interested in her, but she wants no part of it. She keeps pushing him away, which is a shame because he's a good guy. She can't see it though, because she's afraid to get involved again."

I nod. "I can relate. My father walked out on us too. He was never that great, but at least he was *there*. It does mess with the head. If your own parent doesn't love you, then you start to wonder why someone would stick around to love you when they don't even have to."

"Until you found Stephan. He's one smitten kitten if I ever saw one."

I want to agree, but I've seen that cold, calculating look in his eye. "I know he loves me, but there are times when I'm afraid he loves his throne more."

"Impossible. You guys have the love story for the ages. It's the kind that inspires fairy tales."

"At least there's no evil stepmother in this one."

"Unless King Franklin decides to take a wife." Michele closes her book and stands up. "I've got enough to start with. You know that once I get going, I'll probably come up with some other things too. I'll let you know."

"Let me at least feed you before you leave. You must be famished."

"The food is decent here."

I smile. "I won't let Frau Einshuchtern know you said it was only decent. She's likely to bake you into the next shepherd's pie for that. She thinks her cooking is the best in the world."

"It certainly was the highlight of your wedding, other than the dress of course."

I try not to let Michele's words sting. She doesn't mean them to be hurtful, even though they are. They are also not untrue. The wedding and reception were pretty stodgy. The food and dress were my favorite parts as well. Besides marrying Stephan, of course. Our marriage was the best thing to come out of that day, and I must remember that through the rough patches in the road.

It's just that the road is much rougher than I ever anticipated.

I love these moments when it's only the two of us. These times seem elusive lately, slipping through my hands like grains of sand. Even at night we're not always in the same residence. It wasn't as if I didn't know travel would be part of our lives. I think I thought I'd be by Stephan's side more than I am.

I'm trying not to take it personally—always being left behind—but well, I'm taking it personally. Especially when Stephan tells me, "We don't think you're ready."

I want to show him my diploma from Princess Academy, but I don't think he would appreciate it. And even I know enough to know that the reason I'm being kept here isn't because I don't cross my ankles or use the proper fork. It's because of Artem.

That's my husband's son.

Everyone else refers to him as "the boy" or, even worse, "the situation." I once commented that I didn't think he was *Jersey Shore* material, but that joke fell flat. It's not my fault I developed an addiction to terrible American television in those long years when all I did was work and help my mom care for my brother.

I keep asking when Artem is coming for a visit or when we're going to meet him. The icy stares and stilted responses that never really answer the question tell me what I need to know.

They're never going to accept him.

This is unacceptable to me.

I know it's not the same situation, but it brings me right back to how my father reacted when he found out that Tomas had Down syndrome. Other than a few brief moments for awkward photographs, I'm not sure

I ever saw my dad hold him. I will not be married to a man who treats his son like a second-class citizen.

Maybe Stephan doesn't understand. I know his father thinks I'm a closet, or even open, Republicist. An Anti-mon. It's not that at all. It's that I think if you sire a child, you should be responsible for said siring. I'm not sure if siring is even a word, but I know what I mean.

"Stephan, we need to talk."

He looks up from his papers, startled. Even in our private time he's always working. It seems the only time I have his full attention is in bed. While I'm happy for that, it'd be nice to spend some quality time together with our clothes on. "Is something wrong?" His blue eyes darken a bit. I know he loves me. I just think he loves Montabago more.

"It's about Ar ... the situation."

Stephan's eyes close as he takes in a deep breath, exhaling slowly. "What now?"

"It's ..." Oh crap. I can't be losing my nerve. "It's just that this whole thing is bothering me, and not for the reasons you think." Stephan opens his mouth, but I stop him with a wave of my hand. "Please let me speak. First of all, I don't want you to say you're sparing my feelings, which I've heard you use as an excuse in the past for not talking about this. It happened long before you met me. Yes, it bothers me that you were somewhat of a man-whore, but it's not as if I don't have a past as well. We can't do anything about it."

"Did you call me a man-whore?" There's a slight upturn to his mouth.

"Admit it, Stephan. You were. I don't blame you. Well, I do. No one forced you to act like that, but I'm guessing it's a rite of passage for the young and wealthy." I perch on the edge of his desk, my bum covering up some of his important papers.

"I think it's more of a rite of passage, period. It had nothing to do with my wealth."

"Of course it did. And this is where I'm going. I know I've told you some about my home life. You know, obviously, my dad deserted us. Frankly, I'm surprised he hasn't popped back up, trying to get a piece of the pie, like Dominicka is doing. But that's not the point."

"It's not?" Stephan raises his eyebrow playfully and puts his hand on my thigh, slipping it under the hem of my skirt.

"No, the point is that I had to grow up quickly. I was sixteen when he left. I had friends. I had a boyfriend. Then, suddenly, I had to work. I had to take care of Tomas. I no longer was young and carefree. I had to be an adult, all because my dad didn't want to. Didn't want us. Do you know how that makes a child feel when their own father doesn't want them?"

Stephan's hand stills, no longer caressing my leg. He's staring straight ahead, unable to look at me.

"It makes a person—a child—feel worthless. Deserving of nothing. Full of self-loathing and reproach. If only I worked harder. If only I weren't so loud. If only I didn't complain so much. If only I were prettier. If only I were better. It's taken me years not to hear those voices with every single thing I do. You— your love—has been a huge part of it. You've shown me I'm worthy. Which is hard to hold onto sometimes

54

when your father makes it obvious he thinks I'm not. I don't want Artem to feel the way I did. And still sometimes do."

He withdraws his hand slowly. After a few minutes he speaks. "I'm sorry about that. You know it pains me that you feel that way at times. But, unfortunately, some things cannot be helped."

"He's a child. You've missed so much. How can you stand to miss one moment more?" I jump off the desk, spurred by a pit in my stomach.

Stephan swivels his chair to look up at me. "Darling, I want you to know that things will be different with our child. Children. I plan on being hands-on with them. I won't miss a moment."

He takes my hands and looks expectantly. "I can't wait for that time in our life to start. To create something wonderful with you."

"I ... I want that too."

"Do you? You don't sound so sure anymore."

"Once I'm more settled and figure out what I'm doing here, then I'll be ready. But it still doesn't change the fact that you have a son already, and I think he should be a part of our lives."

"It's that sort of compassion and understanding that makes me love you so." And with that he stands and envelops me in his arms, his massive frame dwarfing mine. As he lifts me onto his desk, his lips claim mine, and it is not until later—much later—that I realize he never actually responded to my demand that Artem be included.

Chapter 7

"But they want us to come for a visit. Are you on board with this?"

I'm glad my mom can't see me roll my eyes over the phone. "Yes, Ma, I am. Why wouldn't I be? You haven't been here since the wedding, and that was over four months ago."

"Yes, but Tomas."

"Tomas is Tomas. And I miss him too. I know traveling is hard on him, but if we start talking about it now, he should do fine."

"I know ..." she trails off.

"It sounds like there's a 'but' coming."

"... but I don't want to embarrass you."

"Oh, Ma. Get real. If there's any embarrassing going on, it's by me. They're pretty much keeping me locked up in here, afraid to let me into the public eye for fear I'll say something damaging to the cause."

"Why would they think that? You were brilliant on that show. And in the interviews."

Little does she know that the majority of that was read from the teleprompter. No, King Franklin and his lackeys do not trust what would come out of my mouth. Especially now.

"Things are ... tense ... with the election and all. It's only a little over two months away."

"Just think, because the election is going on in America at the same time, Montabago is hardly getting any world coverage. So how could anything you do really matter?"

I want to tell her about Artem, even though I know her advice would mirror what I've already said. I've promised Stephan I wouldn't say anything. He nearly blew a gasket when he found out I'd talked to Michele about it. At least she's signed confidentiality clauses and whatnot. I think that's the only reason he finally calmed down. Good ole Daniel, reminding Stephan of that fact. I'm not sure if I love Daniel or hate him. He's a good confidant for my husband, but I still can't tell whose interests he's working toward— Stephan's or the palace's.

"And anyway, Daniel thinks it would be a good idea for you and Tomas to visit. To show that the palace is in touch with everyday people."

"Then that would be a no." Her tone is icy. I don't need to ask why. It was my first reaction when Daniel brought it up as well. But then I realized how much I missed Ma and Tomas, and I didn't care about political motivations.

"I know what you're thinking, Ma, because I thought the same thing. I won't let them put you on camera. I just want to see you."

"Then why don't you come here? You've complained about being cooped up in the palace with nothing to do."

"I should if there's room for me."

"Psst, of course there's room. There's always room, especially here."

I knew she was right. The house I'd grown up in, on Coventry Lane, had been quaint but never felt cramped. Three bedrooms. One-and-a-half baths. Kitchen, dining room, family room. A mudroom-laundry combo on the back porch. The apartment the palace had set her up in was at least as big, if not bigger, with fewer people. They have trained staff to help care for Tomas, should my mother desire. I know she's occasionally used this benefit but doesn't abuse it. She tries to get done whatever she needs to while Tomas is at his "job" and only uses the help if she's sick or traveling to visit family.

No one could ever accuse us of being gold diggers.

Yet despite that, I worried it's what people really thought I was about when Stephan and I first started dating. King Franklin has virtually said so. It's fine. I know why I fell in love with Stephan. Although, in this moment of missing my mother and brother so, I wonder if my love for Stephan was a good enough reason for leaving.

I feel as if I deserted them.

Everyone tells me I didn't. My mother is grateful for the luxurious new living accommodations and the help with Tomas. I know her life is now easier because of me. I get that. At least I tell myself I understand that. But I still don't feel ... fulfilled. I tell Ma I'll think about going to visit her if she thinks about coming to visit me and end the phone call feeling even more lonely than before.

I'm thirty-one, almost thirty-two, and I have *nothing* to do most of the time. I'd like to at least be on the board of some charity organizations or something, but I've been advised against doing so until after the election is over. *We don't want to be accused of attempting to sway the vote* is the current palace stance.

I'm no political strategist, but I sort of think it would make the whole monarchy seem more appealing if we were out there helping others, rather than sitting behind the walls each day. I've been thinking on it, and I'd love to help kids afford to go to University. You know, the ones who have to choose between eating and school, like I did.

Which is what I make the mistake of saying at lunch. With my husband. And his father. And Baron Von Windbag, because the two of them are joined at the hip. Daniel is there as well.

The inner circle.

The only thing out of place is me. One of these things is not like the others. And I'll give you a hint: it's probably not because I don't have testicles, although that could be a leading reason why I'm dismissed without a thought.

I've often wondered what it would be like if Stephan's mother, Queen Margarethe, were still alive. Surely she would have brought some balance to this testosterone-driven, "I-am-never-wrong" mentality that dominates these archaic halls. I'd like to think I'd have an ally, but based upon my plebian upbringing, I have a feeling she'd look at me with just as much distaste as her husband does.

As he does this very minute. I wasn't paying attention and he knows it. Probably another reason I'm not good enough to be in this family.

"I'm sorry, are we boring you? Perhaps you'd like to be excused to go get your nails done."

"Father." Stephan's tone is harsh, and for a moment I can see the king he's destined to be. "You will not speak to my wife like that."

"I will if she continues to insult me by sitting here and staring off into space rather than contributing to the conversation."

Next to me, Stephan is practically reverberating with anger. I lay my hand on his arm and speak. "Forgive me, King Franklin. You did catch me in a moment of thought. I was wondering what Queen Margarethe would have to say on this issue."

I know the queen's name is sacred, only spoken in hushed tones and with the utmost reverence. In their eyes, I've batted it about like a balloon at a child's party. A fire swells and then quickly calms in King Franklin's eyes. "She would do what is necessary to continue the monarchy. *Whatever is necessary.*"

His words send a chill down my spine. I do not like where this is going. Not at all.

He continues. "It's the first week in September now. The election is ten weeks away. The timeline is entirely too compact. I'm quite disappointed in you, Stephan. You had one job to do. We all know you're capable, due to that other mess you've created. I will never forgive you for letting the country down like this."

Now I know I haven't been paying sufficient attention. Stephan's head is hanging low as he's staring at his hands, now in tight fists on his knees. I have never seen him like this. I know I'm missing something, and it's not only because I spaced out a little before. There's something bigger going on here. I want to ask but I'm cut off by Baron Von Windbag.

"The doctor has said that next week would be the perfect timing for the procedure. With close monitoring, we should be able to announce at six weeks. It's earlier than we like to announce in most cases, but in the event of a loss, it would likely garner further support."

Oh. Hell. No. They cannot be talking about what I think they're talking about.

I grip the edge of the table, wishing I could snap it in half like the Incredible Hulk. These people will definitely not like me when I'm angry. Stephan places a hand over mine and gives me a pleading look. "We'll discuss this later. I'll explain it to you."

Explain? It's exactly what I think it is.

I rise to my feet, full of indignation. "I don't think so. You will not *explain* anything to me later. This is my body we're talking about, correct? I assume you're turning to medical involvement to guarantee that I'm pregnant the next chance I get?"

King Franklin lets out a slow, condescending clap. At least Daniel has the decency to look embarrassed.

"Stephan has known his whole life that his biggest responsibility would be to produce an heir to keep the Salzach line alive."

"He has," I interject quickly. "Leave my uterus out of it."

The king continues as if I haven't spoken. "A *legitimate* heir. He has known this timeline since before he hit puberty."

"What timeline?" I hear Stephan suck in a breath next to me. I cannot bring myself to even glance in his direction.

"Courting by the age of thirty-one. Engaged at thirty-two. Married at thirty-three. Father at thirty-four, just in time for the election. He, of course, has left everything to the last minute. But, if the implantation doesn't take or succeed, Nigel is right. A loss could bring even more support than an actual baby."

I want to throw up. My knees feel weak, and I grip the table to keep from falling. Things click into place. "So that is why you permitted this marriage. Not because Stephan and I were in love, but because you needed it to happen."

"My boy has always had a rebel heart. He's never wanted to do as he was told. Hence all the indiscretions that have led to the situation. Marrying a commoner from a broken home was his biggest rebellion attempt. Because he'd left it to the last minute, he knew I'd have to accept you. So, here you are. The one thing he always insisted on was a love match. He says that's what this is, but I am not convinced there's not a bit of revenge here."

There's bile in the back of my throat, and the periphery of my vision is clouding. My legs are no longer capable of supporting me as I sink back down into the chair.

"That's right. So now you need to be quiet and do your royal duty. Be good for something."

There are no words.

No polite ones at least.

The king leaves without apology or excuse, Baron Von Windbag—whose first name is apparently Nigel—trailing at his heels like a dog.

Stephan's head is in his hands. Daniel looks as if he's just witnessed a horrific accident. I can only imagine what I look like.

After several moments, Daniel begins to speak. I hold up my hand to silence him. "I highly doubt there's something either one of you could say that would help in this moment."

Daniel tries to speak again and this time my withering glare stops him. Stephan is still silent. I find the strength to rise, my legs shaky but supporting my weight thus far. "I'm guessing you both knew about the ultimatum about Stephan getting married and procreating."

They both nod, in unison, as if they've practiced for the day they were busted.

"And you both knew we'd be expected to spawn immediately."

Again with the nods.

"And you, Stephan, are unwilling to claim your son as your heir."

This time, he's immobile, answering the question.

"Well, then I think you need to get the royal press in order. The election may not be your biggest issue."

Stephan looks at me, raising his eyebrow slightly. He clearly doesn't know where I'm going with this.

"I would think your impending divorce would be your biggest problem at the moment." I turn to walk away. Stephan doesn't move. He *doesn't make a move.*

And that tells me all I need to know.

Chapter 8

Packing doesn't take long. Most of my personal belongings are in storage or still back at Ma's house. Stephan didn't think I'd need much of my "old stuff" anyway. I take the clothes that Michele made for me. No one else can wear them anyway. I doubt I'll have need for the formal gowns and dresses at home.

Home.

I don't know if such a place exists anymore. At least not for me. Ma and Tomas have moved to the city, about twenty miles from where we used to live. Where I'm heading to now.

Retreating like a dog with a tail between its legs.

I may lick my wounds for quite a while, as long as I'm there.

A long while.

I can't believe I was so foolish. So blind. So stupid.

Of course, what else would you expect from an ignorant, uneducated girl? To believe a prince would love a pauper.

It only took a bit of convincing for the head chauffeur to let me take my car out. I told him it was just for a bit and the old sod fell for it. I haven't driven it in almost two years, since just before the engagement was announced. Engagement. Ha. What a farce. After I toss my bags in the trunk I rip the massive ring off my left hand and shove it in my pocket. I want to throw it away but I know I can't. Four point three carats.

How could I have been so stupid?

That thought runs on repeat through my head, over and over and over until the words no longer make any sense. With one hand, I rummage through the console looking for a CD. Finding it, I thrust it in and let Elton John's "Goodbye Yellow Brick Road" flood the car, as if a soundtrack to my own personal movie montage. At least the security detail has replaced my old clunker with a jazzed-up Benz. It's got more electronics than a rocket ship and I don't know how to work a single one, except the CD player. While I'm grateful for a car that runs, I miss my old convertible. I can picture cruising down the road, the wind whipping through my long brown hair. I try rolling the windows down to get the same effect, but my hair keeps blowing in my eyes and now it looks like a rat's nest. I can't even get my fingers through it without getting caught on snarls, so I pull it back into a very un-princess-like messy bun. I know Claudine would be cringing to see my locks so disheveled. Phaedra would be equally distraught to see my face, my eyes red and virtually swollen shut from all the crying. We won't even discuss the prolific amount of mucus pouring forth from my nose.

Based on the sort of day I'm having, an idiot could have predicted what came next, but still, the noise of the front tire popping shocks me. Yes, obviously I would blow a tire. In the middle of nowhere.

I expect the torrential downpour to start any moment, but instead experience unseasonably high heat and humidity, making me sweat profusely as I move my bags out of the trunk in search of the spare.

Some princess I am, changing a tire in the middle of a road to nowhere. I'm glad I wasn't raised in the palace. Maybe Artem is better off for having a normal life. Hopefully he has someone to teach him life skills like this. Mr. Panagogus taught George and me the summer before my dad ran off with his wife. I guess now I know why my dad didn't have the time to teach me himself.

That's neither here nor there. I'm clumsy, removing the jack and tire irons, but I'm pretty sure I remember what to do. I've got this.

Or not. One of the lug nuts is stuck. Like really stuck. Minutes go by as I struggle to make the darn thing budge. Nope. Not one iota. And if I thought I was sweating before …

A sensible person would admit defeat and call for help. I am not sensible. I have not been sensible since I agreed to go on a date with the Crown Prince of Montabago. My lack of sensibility has continued to plague me these last four years, culminating with my decision to do a factory reset on my phone and leave it in the middle of my royal bed.

It seemed like a good idea at the time.

I didn't want Stephan or Daniel to be able to get a hold of me. It won't take them long to find me at my old house, but I figured maybe I'd get a day or two of peace and quiet and get to sob for hours and not have to answer to a single person.

So that leaves me with a flat tire I'm unable to change and without any way of calling for help. I'm hot and disgustingly sweaty, and apparently the mosquitos find me attractive, as they've been all over every centimeter of exposed skin.

If the press could see me now.

Yet, as I sit on the side of the road, slapping my neck, my wrists, my ankles, I feel an inkling of freedom that's eluded me for years.

I don't know who I was trying to kid. I'm not cut out for this princess stuff. The rules. The regulations. The tradition. The isolation.

If I hadn't been so crazy in love with Stephan, I wouldn't have made the sacrifices. And all for what? I guess Ma and Tomas having an easier life has been worth it. I hate to disappoint them and take all the supports away. I wonder if in the settlement, Stephan would agree to keep that up. I don't want anything from him. Nothing for me at least.

I imagine King Franklin is dancing a jig of joy at this moment. The only thing that would prevent his sour face from grinning ear to ear is that he's lost his uterus. *My* uterus. Oh well. I'm sure Baron Von Windbag and Daniel can spin my leaving as a devastation for Stephan and gain the sympathy vote that way.

Thinking about it brings on another round of tears. This time they're of anger, hot and salty, streaming down my face. I pick up the tire iron and begin hitting the ground. Over and over, screaming like a banshee, until my arms can lift it no more, and I drop to the ground, spent.

"I'm not sure what that piece of soil did to you, but I'm guessing it deserved it."

I jump clear off the ground, startled by the voice behind me. Oh God, I'm going to die. And I don't even have the strength to wield the tire iron in my own defense. I can only imagine what I look like, other than potential prey. Five-foot-one. Small-ish frame. A wild mane of brown hair that looks as if I've been electrocuted, escaping from the top knot on my head. Old flannel shirt (I'm sorry, Michele). Faded jeans. Sneakers. We won't even get into how I probably smell. Maybe that alone will keep me safe.

I don't know whether to pray this person recognizes me or to pray that he doesn't. Either way, if I survive, I'll die of embarrassment.

Slowly I turn toward the voice of my savior or slayer.

And now I wish for death.

What are the odds?

Of all of the gin joints in all the towns in all the world ...

"Hey, George."

"Wow, Maryn. You look ..."

I grip the tire iron a bit tighter and raise my eyebrow. "Think carefully. I'm in a very poor mood."

"So nothing has changed then."

I deserve the bitter tone with which he's addressing me. I know I do. But I have no patience for it.

"I can't get my nut to move."

I try to ignore the grin that dances across his face for a split second. "That sounds like a personal problem, Princess." The edge and bite are back to his voice.

"I've got ninety-nine problems, and the nut's just one." I'm tired. Too tired to deal with this. "Please don't make it one hundred."

George steps forward, not cocky but confident, taking the tire iron from my hand. I see him smile at the tire until he tries to turn the lug nut. And tries. And tries.

And the damn thing still won't budge.

If I had any sense of humor left at all, I'd laugh. Okay, even without a sense of humor, the situation still strikes me as ridiculously funny. George is not amused by my stubborn lug nut and even less so by my cackling, which has now turned maniacal. It continues to evolve further until it turns into sobs. Loud, wracking sobs that leave me gasping for air.

And let's not forget the mucus. So. Much. Mucus.

I've sunk to my knees in the dirt on the side of the road, barely noticing the gravel pressing into them. But still, it's too much effort to maintain this pose and I slide down to a fetal position.

Yes I, Princess Maryn, am lying on the side of the road like a dead animal.

I don't feel much like a princess. Not that I ever did.

"That's part of the problem. I never felt like one," I say, to no one in particular.

But George doesn't know I've apparently gone off the deep end, so he responds, "What problem? What didn't you feel like?"

"It's not me. It's not who I am. They don't know me."

"Who does?"

I don't like his tone, so I sit up and glare at him through puffy, painful eyes. "What's that supposed to mean?"

"You know."

Of course I know, but I'm in the mood to fight. Something I couldn't do with my husband. So George will have to do. "No, I don't."

"Who does know you? Do you even know yourself?"

Since a witty comeback fails to pop into my exhausted brain, I do the next best thing. I stick my tongue out at him.

"Oh, how very elegant of you. Did they teach you that in the palace? In *Princess Academy*?" The disdain drips from his voice.

"How did you know about Princess Academy?" That was my name for it. Valentia and my handlers didn't appreciate it. Nor did Stephan, although he did give me a wan smile from time to time when I'd talk about it. I was strictly forbidden from mentioning it in public.

"Your mother told my father."

I didn't know Ma was still in contact with Mr. Panagogus. It makes sense. She only moved to the apartment two years ago, just before our engagement was announced. Why wouldn't she keep in touch with the man she'd lived next door to for almost forty years? That's what decent human beings do.

"Yeah, well, that's not supposed to be said in public, so if you wouldn't mind keeping that quiet."

"Because yes, I would be at your beck and call, *Your Highness*, wouldn't I? I've nothing better to do than wait around for you to deem me worthy of your presence."

I want to scream and shout that he's wrong. But he's not. Of course he's not. My etiquette coaches would be horrified at how I've acted toward George.

I'm horrified.

I finally bring my gaze to George's. I feel my cheeks burn with color as I look at the face I once knew as well as my own. But now it's filled with lines and stubble, and even a small scar on his eyebrow that didn't used to be there. But those green eyes are the same. And different all at the same time.

Because they used to look at me with adoration, and now are filled with hate.

I get it. I deserve it.

I'm loyal like my father. Which is not at all.

"Okay then, well thanks for stopping. I appreciate you trying to help. I guess I'll just stay here then."

"Don't be ridiculous. Get in my car. Where are you going?"

"Can I take my stuff?"

"What stuff?"

I point to the pile of bags I'd emptied out to access the spare.

"Again, where are you going?"

"Home."

"Your car is pointed in the opposite direction. The palace is that way." He nods in the direction from which I've just come.

"You know what I mean." I pick up my bags, trying unsuccessfully to carry all three at once.

George lets out a huff and picks up two of the bags, tossing them as if they weigh nothing, into his trunk. I add the third and then grab one last bag out of the front seat. I look and there's nothing left of value in my car. The car belongs to the palace, so at this point, if someone makes off with it, I don't care. Once I get home, I'll call someone about towing it. There's a lot more on my mind than a stupid car.

Plus, once I get home I'm not leaving unless I have to.

"So, home ...?" We've been sitting in an uncomfortable silence for twenty minutes. Home is rapidly approaching, the hills becoming familiar. Coventry Lane is in the middle of farmland, our two houses close together, with the next neighbors out of sight. Legend has it that our houses were part of a larger estate, built for the children of the landlord. Twins who didn't want to be separated. For the first sixteen years of my life, I thought it was great to have the Panagoguses so close. After all, George was my best friend.

Was.

I don't answer his question, too lost in my own thoughts. I forget he's even asked a question. That is until he slams the car to a stop in front of my dark house. He gets out and opens the trunk. I hear my bags hit with a thud. One. Two. Three. I remain in my seat, unable to move. I can't believe my life has come to this. Finally, George yanks open my door and gives a mocking bow as I exit. "Good to know you haven't changed a bit. I thought with all that smiling and waving, kissing babies and accepting flowers, maybe you had softened. It's nice to know that even all the riches in the country can't change your heart of stone."

Before I can blink, he's back in the car, pulling out, leaving me standing in darkness facing my childhood home.

Chapter 9

When I was a little girl, my mom was never a big proponent of fairy tales. Therefore, predictably, I couldn't get enough. I wanted to dress like Cinderella, complete with fancy ball gowns and carriages. I couldn't figure out why my mom objected so. What could be wrong with that?

When I was thirteen, just after Tomas was born, my mother finally told me. Holding a fussy baby, short on sleep and so completely frazzled, she looked at me and said, "Don't hold out for the prince on the white horse to sweep in to the rescue. You need to be your own savior. Never rely on someone else to save you."

I looked at her and said, "But George will always be there to save me."

Those words echo in my head, mocking me. I believed it at the time. I was going to marry George and we were going to build a house on the back lot, just out of our parents' sight. He would farm the land, and I would be there cooking and reading and knitting. But that was before the floor dropped out and I became a horrible human being.

And then, of course, I did meet a prince. No, he didn't have a white horse. Well, he does actually have one for polo; just not for everyday savior things. But for a while, it did seem as if he was sweeping in and solving all my problems.

But damn it all if Ma wasn't right. He wasn't my salvation. He was my condemnation. A life sentence. Because I would be fertile.

Or at least they hoped I would be.

I can't believe I was so foolish to believe that he loved me for me. For my personality. And here I was, thinking I was moving up in the world. Proving to my father that I didn't need him and that I could become something in spite of him.

Spite. I didn't realize Stephan chose me to spite his father.

And every time I think about this my heart breaks all over again.

I get that I wasn't cut out to be a member of the royal family. It was a lot harder than I ever thought. Certainly more than dresses and Champagne and smiling for the cameras.

I feel like I may never smile again.

Especially considering that there's no electricity in the house. I'm disgustingly dirty, now cold, and sitting in the dark. Of course there's no electricity. Why would it still be on? Ma doesn't live here anymore. There's a thin layer of dust, though I would have expected more. Someone must have been in here to clean in the not-too-distant past. I wonder if Ma brought Tomas out. It's his job to dust and vacuum. Ma felt strongly that he have some life skills. It takes him a long time but he does a thorough job. Instantly

I'm brought back to the days, years ago when it was the three of us, both Ma and me, showing Tomas. Taking his hand and moving it, dusting the table. Repeating the same things over and over. It may have taken a while but he got it.

I miss her. I miss him. I even miss the days when life was hard. Because it was simple. Nothing's going to be simple again.

I feel my way into the kitchen, along the cabinets, and to the sink. I pray that the water is still on. For once in this terrible week, luck is with me. Not enough that there's hot water, but the cold water feels refreshing on my swollen face.

Thank God it was George who found me on the side of the road. First of all, he already hates me, so it's not as if he's going to pass judgment. Secondly, he's not going to call the paparazzi to come and take pictures of me looking like a train wreck. Third, he's not going to be up in my grill, wanting a piece of the fame that goes along with being royalty. Being married to royalty. Once having been married to royalty.

I can't believe we're getting divorced after four months. I feel like a Kardashian.

It's not as if I thought I'd be on par with Diana or Kate Middleton. Most people outside of our tiny little corner of the world had never even heard of the United Republic of Montabago until *Made for Me* premiered. And even then ... well at least the Google hits for Montabago increased exponentially. But this scandal is sure to make me a laughing stock.

I take a long drink of cold water, promptly refilling my glass. My throat feels like it's made of sandpaper, and I'm sure that I'm dehydrated. There can't be much fluid left in my body at all since it all poured forth from my eyes.

The night deepens, plunging me into total darkness. The palace never gets this dark. And the thought hits me. I'm totally screwed.

I don't know what's left in the house, but I know what's not here. Ma threw out all the candles and matches, afraid that Tomas would burn the house down. And while I've got water so I won't die of dehydration, I doubt there's any edible food. And there's no heat. And no phone. And no car.

I did not think this through.

The way I see it, I've only one option.

But it's not an option. My pride will not let it be an option.

Damn my pride.

I need to go over to the Panagogus's house for help. Maybe George doesn't live there anymore. Why would he? I'm sure he's got his own place. His dad might help me. While I'm sure he's not my biggest fan, he might not hate me as much as George does.

Not that I blame George. I'd hate me too.

I've got a lot of hate and anger at the moment. And it's pretty exhausting. Let's face it, I'd probably kill myself trying to walk across the field to George's house. I feel my way into the hall and up the stairs. One door, wall space. Second door, wall space. Then finally to the linen closet. The smell of mothballs and cedar wafts out, instantly bringing back a simpler time. Building a fort in my grandmother's cedar closet. Hiding from George in this very closet. I feel around, finding some old blankets. I haul them out and feel my way back to my old room. The smell consumes me as I pile the blankets on top of me, enveloping me in their warmth. I feel like I'm in a cocoon where nothing bad could possibly happen. If only it were true.

I must be dreaming because I smell coffee. It can't be true because there's no food and no electricity in the house. My mind must be playing tricks on me. Maybe I've finally gone off the deep end. It would be justified.

Alas, I'm not going crazy. There really is coffee. I know this because George walks into the room, carrying a mug, which steams in the cold room. The temperature must have dropped precipitously after the unseasonably warm day yesterday. I don't remember September normally being this cold, but I've never really spent too much time in a domicile without electricity. It's not as if my dad was the type to take me camping or anything.

I know without even looking that the coffee will be the perfect shade of brown, enough milk to take away the bitterness. And milk, not cream. Just enough sugar.

He knows me. He knows how I take my coffee. I'm not sure Stephan does. It's not as if he's ever made me a cup, and it's not likely he would, even if I hadn't shunned the beverage that reminds me of my father. I'm sure, if we were normal people, he would. It's that, well, we're not typical. At least Stephan's not. I'm not sure he knows *how* to make a cup of coffee, let alone one specific to my palate.

He's too busy running a country.

And denying his son. And trying to get me to produce the next heir. I groan and pull the pillow over my face, not wanting this to be my reality.

On the other hand, George doesn't realize I no longer drink coffee. So much has changed since we were together.

George huffs and turns back out of the room. I hear him stomping away. What I don't hear is him putting the coffee down, so I peek out from underneath my pillow.

Crap.

I'm not supposed to say that, but I do. Well, at least in my head I think it.

I haul myself out of the cocoon of blankets and shiver. Although I'd never say it out loud, I'm missing the luxuries of the palace. You know, heat. Hot water. A warm croissant.

George is nowhere to be seen. My coffee is on the floor at the top of the stairs, steam no longer visible. It's cold, like me. I try to ignore the chill underneath my feet and make a mental note to dig out some socks as soon as possible. I wonder if George would let me take a shower at his house. It's too much to ask. A cold shower can't be that bad.

I was wrong. A cold shower is that bad. Holy shnikeys. On the other hand, I've never cleaned up so quickly. I didn't even bother with the conditioner and there may still be shampoo in my hair. My clothes are clean and dry, so that's an improvement.

But that's about it. I'm going to have to go to George for help. He's the only neighbor in walking distance. I really made some poor decisions, getting rid of my phone, leaving the car, abandoning my husband. It's not like I wanted to abandon him. There were some deal breakers, and now I have to live with it and so will he.

The only thing that makes this drama maybe somewhat tolerable is the fit I imagine King Franklin pitching. His face, more crimson than his royal robes. Not that I've ever seen him wear royal robes, this being the twenty-first century and all, but I imagine he has them, lined in ermine. I bet he parades around his chambers wearing them and a crown and nothing else.

But even that comical image won't help me out of my current predicament. Especially—oh God, I hadn't thought about this—if George won't help me. What will I do then?

Of course he'll help me. It's George. It's what George does. He already gave me a ride and brought me coffee.

But I can tell from the hard glares and the set of his jaw that he hasn't forgiven me. It's understandable. I haven't forgiven myself, no matter how long it's been.

Destroying a person will have that effect on you. And whether I want to admit it or not, that's what I did to George. He didn't deserve it. I know that. I knew that. But I was hurting so I lashed out.

I'm not proud of it. In fact, it's the only regret in my life. Well, I guess I now have two. Regrets or not, it's time to tuck my tail between my legs and eat some humble pie for breakfast.

I don't have to go far, as George is out at the fence line. Yes, a fence separates our properties. It never kept George and me apart. I guess it didn't keep my dad from diddling his mom either. Some fence.

"Thank you for the coffee. I ... uh ... really ... thanks." I don't know why I'm tripping and falling over my words. It's only George. I lean on the post.

"I didn't think you could lower yourself enough to thank me." He doesn't even look up from what he's doing, which is working on some sort of electrical box. I wonder if the fence is now electrified and if, at any moment, a surge of current will zap through my body. Maybe I should take a step back.

"What do you mean by that? You threw my stuff out yesterday before I could thank you. I do appreciate the help."

"Anyone would have stopped," he says gruffly, continuing to work without meeting my gaze.

"Yes, maybe. But most people would have made it public first chance they got. I'm guessing that wasn't your first priority."

"No, I went home and got loaded and waited for you to come over."

His words hang heavy in the air, and I know he's talking about so much more than last night. He's been waiting since I was sixteen. Almost half my life.

"I'm sorry."

"Sorry for what?"

I know everything I should say, but those words are nearly impossible in this moment. I don't have the strength to go through it. "Aww, c'mon George. You know what I mean."

Now he finally looks at me, those green eyes piercing down to my very core. "No, I'm afraid I don't know what you mean."

I take a deep breath. I can do this. Here goes nothing. "I'm sorry about ... what I did all those years ago. I was wrong. I was acting from a place of hurt, where I felt betrayed and disappointed. I took it out on you. I never once considered that you might be feeling the same way. I never once considered that you might need me. Instead, I shut you out. It was wrong, and how I acted was inexcusable. I've come to terms with those facts. I don't hope that you can forgive me. I only hope that you're still the decent person you were all those years ago and can look past my shortcomings and provide me with some assistance."

A moment passes. Two moments pass. I can't look away. I'm not one to make grand gestures or sweeping apologies. George finally breaks my stare and starts walking toward my house. It takes me a moment to realize that not only did he not accept my apology, but he didn't even acknowledge it! Finally, I start running after him, my short legs working overtime to catch up with his brisk pace. He's not as tall as Stephan, but he moves with an urgency that makes up for his lack of height. Enough so that I'm out of breath by the time I catch up to him at the back door.

He walks in like he owns the place and flips a switch. The lights flicker on, illuminating the kitchen. I almost wish they hadn't, as the worn out dinginess is on full display in the glare of the bright florescent lights. Seeing the kitchen lit up is like seeing myself. Being in the palace, I was cloaked in dark where all you could tell was that I had the right pieces. Seeing them on display with light beaming down—I'm just like this kitchen. Dingy, dirty, and I'll never be good enough.

Chapter 10

Oh crap, here come the tears again. George looks over at me and rolls his eyes.

"I swear, I never cry like this. I just ... it's too much."

I expect him to ask or say something quasi-supportive or sympathetic, but then I remember how I treated him and that I don't deserve anything from him. Furiously, I wipe the tears away. "Thank you for getting the electric running again. Thank you for the ride and the coffee as well. I'm sorry to have put you out."

He turns away and pauses at the back door. I take a good look. A last look. His body is different than it was the last time I saw him. Now it's that of a man. When I was sixteen and he seventeen, he was well built. Now ... wow. His shoulders are broad on his narrow frame, and I'd place bets about the muscles underneath.

"You've changed." The words are out of my mouth before I know it. I'm not generally impulsive. Perhaps my friendship with Michele has caused a little of her to rub off on me.

George turns to face me. "You're one to talk. I don't know who you are anymore. I haven't known for a long time. The person I used to know is long gone."

"Yes, I'm different. I hope to God I'm not the same foolish person I was at sixteen."

The hurt in his face is apparent. "I guess that makes me the fool for loving that girl."

I knew he loved me. He said it often. And I loved him. Just because I broke his heart and acted like a cruel and heartless wench didn't mean I stopped loving him. Quite the contrary, actually.

It took me years to get over George Panagogus.

The person who finally healed me and taught me to trust again was Stephan. Yeah, if that's not irony, I don't know what is.

"Let's say that I'm perhaps not the best judge of character. I seem to trust the wrong people and distrust the right people."

I see George's shoulders sag for an instant before he squares his posture. I need to continue before he interrupts.

"What I did to you, George, was wrong. I'm sorry. That's what I was trying to apologize for this morning."

"All the king's horses and all the king's men can't put Humpty Dumpty back together again."

And he leaves. Yet again. Why is he always leaving me? Why does he keep coming back? I sort of wish he'd stay gone. When he's not in front of me, I can forget about how he used to make me laugh. How he'd hold my hand when I was scared. How he smelled. How he felt.

Then I remember how his face looked when I told him I would never forgive his mother for what she'd done and how I didn't want anything to do with anything associated with her. Including him.

It never occurred to me that he was probably dealing with similar feelings and was willing to work past his hatred of my father. Unlike me. He was, and probably still is, the better person.

Then, despite the fact that we still attended school together, I did not speak to him again. No matter how many times I saw him I looked the other way, holding my chin up high like a snot. Usually I was trying not to remember what his mouth felt like on mine and how our bodies fit together perfectly. After a few years, I did manage to forget.

Then I met Stephan and convinced myself that George was nothing more to me than a childhood playmate.

I am such a liar.

If he didn't matter, I wouldn't have invited him to the wedding. Yes, I put his name on the list. I wanted him to know I'd moved on and I'd done better. That I'd risen above the trash our families represented. What a fool.

King Franklin has every right to treat me the way he does. I'm nothing more than the rubbish he thinks I am.

I sit at the worn kitchen table contemplating my next move. I really shouldn't have left my phone behind. I'm not used to being this isolated. And I keep pissing George off, and he's my only contact to the outside world.

If I can get my car, I'll be fine. I can get groceries and hole up here for a while. At least until the election is over.

Oh my God, I can watch TV again! I rush to the den and make myself comfortable on the couch. The old afghan is still there, bringing back memories of a simpler, happier time. Times with my mom and Tomas. A time when I was surrounded by love and laughter. I focus back on the TV. That was banned in the palace. I think mostly because they don't want to know what the rags are saying about them. Which was odd, considering the powers that be came up with the whole concept of me going on a television show. I bet someone—probably Daniel—urged my participation to help modernize perception of the palace and connect with a younger audience. They probably had creative control over it. I know for my limited dialogue I had scripts and question banks that I had to memorize. The only ones aloud to speak off-the-cuff were the designers.

And now I can find out what the people really think of the election process.

Three hours later, I click the television off, my head pounding. Now I know why things were so tense in the palace.

This is not looking good for the Salzach monarchy. Not at all. The general consensus is that King Franklin is the old guard, out of touch with the current global issues facing his tiny country. Whether to stay in the European Union or to leave with Britain. The stance on the influx of immigrants from Syria. Cyberterrorism. Even the goings on in America. The currency of Montabago is weak at the moment. Republicists want a parliamentary system of elected officials.

Frankly, the pundits are so confident that the monarchy will lose the election that candidates are already running for Parliament. Per the constitution that rules the land, should the people choose not to renew the monarchy as the ruling body, an election will be held three weeks following the main election day. The monarchy will hold power through that time to prevent chaos from descending.

No wonder King Franklin and Baron Von Windbag think nothing of using me and my uterus to gain sympathy and the common vote. I almost don't blame them.

Almost.

There's nothing about an impending royal divorce. That would be the nail in the coffin, so I'm sure they're trying to keep it on the D.L. It's not as if I was seen on a daily basis or had any vital role.

Other than being fertile, obviously.

Granted we've only been married a few months, but I could have been out there, helping the monarchy's cause. Talking to people. I'm fairly certain that I can relate to the commoners a lot better than King Franklin or even Stephan can.

If only Stephan weren't a prince then maybe we would have had a shot. But after watching channel after channel I know we never stood a chance. Because it's not about us. It's about the country. And after all I went through with my father, I can't tolerate playing second fiddle.

To Stephan, we're all second. Montabago is first and always will be.

So now I need to figure out what I'm going to do post-marriage.

I haven't got a clue what I'm going to do for the rest of the day, let alone the rest of my life.

About mid-afternoon, my car arrives. Of course it does, because George took care of it without me even asking.

I hate him in this moment. He's so freakin' perfect. Can't he have one stinkin' flaw? I don't need in-depth analysis to know that my anger toward George is because he makes me feel bad about myself. If the situation were reversed, I'm not sure I'd lift a finger to help him.

I've got tons of time to examine my substandard moral code, but that won't put food in the house. I grab a hat and sunglasses and head out. Going into town would be easiest, but I'd rather fly as far under the radar as I can. I stand a good chance of not being recognized. First of all, I'm not supposed to be here. My mother doesn't live here anymore. I should be in the palace. Second, without the magical intervention of Phaedra and Claudine, I barely look like me. Well, the *me* the public knows. Plus, instead of one of my chic Michele originals, I'm in jeans and a long sweater. My hair is in a careless braid.

One last look in the mirror tells me I bear only the faintest resemblance to Princess Maryn. Which is good. And bad. While I know I'm not cut out for the pomp and circumstance of royalty, I'm not sure I'm this grungy, frumpy girl anymore either.

The swollen eyes and blotchy face don't help. I haven't cried this much since I was sixteen. Stupid men in my life, making me cry. A hat and sunglasses complete my disguise.

I drive the forty-five minutes to Castelo, constantly scanning through the radio stations. Trying to avoid those that play love songs, of course. I even try to avoid the news but end up listening anyway. There are some monarchy supporters still out there. Those who love the *tradition*. If I hear the word tradition one more time I'm going to scream. Tradition means my husband won't recognize his son. Tradition means I have to stand whenever my father-in-law enters or exits the room even though he shows no respect for me as a human being.

What gets me the most is Stephan. At least King Franklin is consistent with his disdain for me. Stephan acts like a totally different person in private as compared to when he's on "royal duty." He's so subservient to his father. He acts like more of a lackey than someone who's second-in-command.

Part of me—the very small part that's not furious with Stephan—aches for him. I know how it is to want your father's approval but to never be good enough. I know more than anyone how hard Stephan works. And how much he loves his country.

He loves Montabago more than his wife.

That thought threatens to bring on a new deluge of tears, but since I have to enter a store I try to hold back. I haven't been shopping in ages. I check my purse. There's some cash in there. Not much. I'm not sure what happened to my credit cards. I suppose some loyal palace staffer has them—if they're even still open.

Now I have to hold back the bitter, and most likely maniacal, laugh that threatens to erupt as I stroll up and down the aisles, basket over my arm as if I don't have a care in the world. Here I am, a freakin' *princess*, and I'm back to buying ramen noodles and canned tuna. This time I don't even have the benefit of coupons to offset the cost.

This money thing is going to be a real problem, one I hadn't thought about. Before I can think about a more long-term solution, a hand grabs my elbow and whips me back toward the endcap where we're hidden by a display. I'm going to die.

"What do you think you're doing?" George hisses, peering out from under his own cap and sunglasses. He's angled me close to him, our sides pressed together, his grip firm on my arm.

"What do I think I'm doing? What are you doing here? How did you know I was here? What did you do, follow me?"

He gives me a quick glance and then pretends to study the can of whatever it is that he's picked up off the shelf. I'm sure, to the casual observer, we're a close couple who is very interested in the nutritional content of our food.

"You did follow me, didn't you?"

"Why didn't you go into town?" he hisses. I'm trying to ignore the vice-like grip he has on my arm. It's starting to hurt, but I can't let him know that.

"I didn't want anyone to know I was back. Or that I'm not where I'm supposed to be."

"Speaking of, why aren't you there?"

The last thing I want to do is get into it in the middle of a grocery. "It's complicated."

"Does he know where you are?"

"I don't want to talk about it."

"I'm taking that as a no since you don't have a security detail with you. I followed you here, and you had no clue until my hands were on your body. What if I were some deranged anti-mon looking for a way to make a statement?"

The super overdramatic part of me wants to reply that it would be what Stephan and the king deserve for treating me the way they did, but even I know that's not true. At least not for Stephan. "I'm fine. No one here recognizes me."

"That's because you look terrible." He looks down at my basket and its meager contents and sighs. "Some things never change, do they?"

"If you mean the fact that I don't have much money, then yes. Who would have thought the princess would actually be a pauper?"

Finally George lets go of my elbow, only to press a set of keys into my hand. "Blue truck. Go get in, keep your head down, and lock the doors. I'll get you some ... real food ... and be out in a moment." Before I can argue, he takes the basket off my other arm and heads down the aisle.

I follow George's instructions, partly because I think he's right but mostly because I'm used to following directions these days. The monarchy is truly antiquated if it strips a woman not only of control over her body but the ability to think.

I don't see any way I can ever return to the palace. Which means I can't go back to Stephan no matter how many tiny pieces my heart has shattered into.

Time escapes me. I don't know if it's been fifteen seconds or fifteen minutes when George raps on the driver's side window. I unlock the door, my shaking hands fumbling with the lock. Wordlessly, he pulls the seat forward, puts the bags in the back, and then returns the seat to upright. He climbs in and starts the motor without a word.

"Oh, wait! My car is here. We can't leave. I need to drive."

George puts the truck in park. "Go ahead. I'll follow you back. Make sure I'm behind you the whole time. Don't try to speed ahead. This girl here can only go so fast, and you seem to have a lead foot."

I wish I didn't have my stupid car, only so I wouldn't have to be alone for the drive back. I peer into the mirror to verify George's beat-up old truck is still behind me. How did I not notice it on the way out?

Because, once again, I was absorbed in Stephan, even if it was only radio coverage. George is right. There could have been a stalker or an anti-mon or a foreign terrorist, and I never would have seen them.

I wonder how George would feel about a private security detail for the foreseeable future?

Chapter 11

"You need a plan."

I know George is trying to be helpful, and let's face it, I've needed the help, but I don't like being told what to do. In fact, I outright resent it. "You need to stop telling me what to do. Everyone needs to stop telling me what to do. Maryn, sit here. Maryn, don't fidget. Maryn, stay awake. Maryn, get pregnant." With each statement, I slam something. The cupboard door, the kitchen dish towel, the can of soup. When I have a ceramic bowl in my hand, George calmly steps in front of me and grasps my wrist.

"No need to shatter a dish over this."

"Right." I look at his hand on my wrist, steadying it. I know if he lets go the bowl would be shaking with my anger. "Right." I put the intact bowl on the counter and step back. "It was my grandmother's."

"I know. You wouldn't want to break it."

I look at the blue speckled ceramic. "It has no value. Certainly nothing monetary."

"Isn't that the bowl she used for your soup when you were sick?"

I nod, smiling at the memory. My heart hurts, missing Mim more than I can say in this moment. "I wonder why Ma left it here."

"She left enough here so she and Tomas can come out and be comfortable when they want. I turn on the power and they're good to go."

"Oh." It would explain a lot, especially the lack of dust. I can't believe I didn't know that they still come here. "How often are they out?"

"About once a month. Tomas earns trips 'home' for hard work."

And just when I thought I couldn't feel any worse, I do. While I knew my decision to marry Stephan impacted Ma and Tomas, I thought it was for the better. Apparently I've ruined their lives as well. My legs give out as I slide down the cabinets to the floor. "Everything's ruined. It's a mess. It's all my fault."

George sits down beside me and, without saying a word, slides an arm around my shoulder, pulling me close. We used to do this all the time until I destroyed our love. But in this moment, our history doesn't seem to matter. George is here for me as he always was.

What would have happened if I hadn't pushed him away?

I bolt upright and move away from George's comfort. I cannot be thinking this way. I'm married. And not to the man sitting on the floor next to me.

George's arm recoils, and he's on his feet before I can say anything. The slump to his shoulders betrays his hurt. Damn it. I've done it again.

"No, George, wait! I didn't mean it like that!"

"Didn't you?" His look is cold. Removed.

"No. I ... I was ... it's not you."

There's no mistaking the bitterness in his laugh. "Are you really going to use the 'it's not you, it's me' line?"

"But it is 'me.' I'm married. I shouldn't be finding comfort in the arms of another man."

"I thought your marriage was over."

"It is. Well, not technically yet. And until it is, I'm still ... well, I'm still the princess. Royal protocol prohibits being touched and touching in public."

"Are you serious?"

"Yes. We're not allowed public displays of affection, and no one is allowed to touch us."

George looks at me for a moment. "That's like the dumbest thing I've ever heard."

"Oh, there are tons more stupid things. And I learned them all."

"Princess Academy?"

I nod. "Yes. It was nowhere near as easy as watching *The Princess Diaries* led me to believe. I thought it would be a cakewalk because my eyebrows were in better shape than the main character's, and I didn't wear Doc Martens."

"Okay, so I'm not allowed to touch you. Got it. Anything else I should know about, Your Highness?"

The tone of his voice makes me uneasy. The friendly George who saved Mim's soup bowl from my destructive anger is gone. I suppose it's what I deserve. I'm a horrible person for what I did to him all those years ago.

"George, you have to let me apologize. You're here, being so nice. You keep helping me out even though you must hate me. You help my mom out. I don't deserve it."

"No, Maryn, you don't."

"Then why are you doing it?"

"Because, no matter what your title is, I'm better than you, and I want you to remember it."

His words sting, mostly because they're true. "I know. What I did ... back then ... it wasn't right."

George takes a seat at the worn and marred kitchen table while I resume making my soup. I lift the can toward him, a peace offering, but he shakes his head to decline the offer. "You know, I can almost forgive what you did back then. We were young. Our lives had been turned upside down. I can kind of understand. There was too much going on between our families for us to be able to work out. The dick move was the wedding invite."

He's completely right about that, but still, I choke on the words. "You're not incorrect."

"Why, Maryn? Jesus, why? It's not as if I didn't know. I mean, I still live next to your mother. Plus, it's not like you could hide it. The town's been crawling with paparazzi since you went public. And then, that stupid television show. I, well, it wasn't the person I thought I knew. But I guess you aren't now are you?"

"You're right. I know I shouldn't have sent it. I didn't need to prove myself to you. There was only one person I wanted to stick it to."

"I'm not him."

"I know. But I can't seem to separate you from him."

"Jesus, Maryn. Get over it! It was years ago. Yes, my mother was screwing your father. So were a lot of other women. It's not like he was ever discreet about it. The only people who didn't seem to know were you and your mom. Or maybe you turned a blind eye. Whatever the case, I'm not the reason he left. And *I'm not him* so stop punishing me like I am."

George is out the door before I can say anything. He's right. Of course he's right. God, I am so bad at this. No wonder my marriage is already over.

Speaking of which, I wonder what Stephan thinks about my absence. Has he even noticed I'm gone? Does he miss me?

I've got so much swirling through my head. Stephan. Babies. The throne. Artem. Ma and Tomas. That last one is perhaps the hardest to deal with. I thought I was making their lives better. I should have realized that Tomas wouldn't like the change. Now I'm not sure if Ma did either.

When I was working twelve- and fourteen-hour days between the laundry and the cafeteria, I never thought I'd utter these words. Money doesn't make life better.

Crap. Well, what am I going to do now?

Truth be told, I've got nothing.

George is right. I do need a plan. Of course, I'd rather get a Brazilian wax than admit that to him. Or anyone. As much as I resented the tight reins the palace staffers had me in, it was nice to know what was expected of me and what each day was going to entail. That was pretty nice. I didn't have to think.

Let's face it, I haven't had time to think since my dad left. The last thing I thought about was that I couldn't stand to be around George anymore, and I'd pretend he didn't exist. Thinking was a luxury I no longer had. I couldn't think about what I wanted to be when I grew up. Who I wanted to marry. Where I wanted to live. Nope. All I could do was make it from one moment to the next. Work. Chores. Tomas. Repeat.

There wasn't time to dream. To want. Frankly, all I wanted was a day off to sleep and read. To get lost in someone else's world for a bit. And to not smell like grease and fabric softener, which, by the way, is not a good combination.

I didn't know what I wanted to do when I was fifteen. All I wanted was to be with George forever and ever. If you'd asked me back then, I probably would have said I wanted to be a wife and mother. That's it. It was good enough for my mom.

But it wasn't. And I was stupid not to have any aspirations of my own. Look where it landed me. Qualified to do nothing but be a wife and mother, and probably not even that. What sort of advice would I give? Crap all over the people who mean the most. Run away when things get hard. Let people make you feel as if you're not good enough.

Future mother of the year, right here.

Maybe I should be a poet.

Except everything I try to write starts with, "There once was a man from Nantucket."

I know I can wait tables and serve food and clean other people's clothes. It may not be glamorous, but at least I was competent. King Franklin will probably pass a stone when the media hits on this one. I can just see it: *Rags to Riches to Rags*. At least I'll be true to myself.

Whoever that is.

For about the billionth time in the past twenty-four hours, I curse myself for being so brazen—a.k.a. stupid—in leaving my phone behind. Ma cut the phone service to the house when Stephan and I first started dating. She was getting harassed. And no way in hell am I going over to George's to ask to use his phone. I'd rather die first.

But I'm also restless and need something to calm my nerves. I scan through the books on the shelf in the living room, but nothing jumps out at me. Plus, I've read them all before. That was the one hobby I had. The one thing I truly enjoyed. Reading.

Maybe I should become a librarian. Or better yet, work in a bookstore. But still, I'm too on edge to read. Hanging on the back of the spindle chair is one of Ma's bags of yarn. She was always knitting something. She taught me but I never loved it the way she did.

I look in the bag and there are a few untouched skeins of yarn as well as needles and several sheets of paper with patterns on them. I read through the patterns until I find a relatively simple one that makes sense to me. Casting the yarn on, I feel the tension seep out of my shoulders and down into my right foot. Weird habit, curling the toes of my right foot under when I knit. I did it at nineteen and I still do it now. No worries. It's me and the yarn and my plan to work in a bookstore.

All I need are some cats and I'm on my way to being that crazy old lady. Far cry from princess. Which certainly wasn't all it was cracked up to be.

But that's A-okay with me.

Chapter 12

My gown makes a crinkling noise with each step I take. Even with the slightest breath there's a faint rustling. I turn to look at the back of the dress and the swooshing sound makes me jump. No matter the sound, the frock is a work of art, and I feel honored to have it on my body.

"Michele, you've really outdone yourself this time." I mean it too. Except for that damn rustling noise. Clothes shouldn't have their own soundtrack. It's almost as bad as the zipping sound my corduroys used to make as I ran round as a careless kid.

"I didn't know how it would all turn out, but I'm like totally in love with it. I can't even."

"I'm sure you can't." Michele says that all the time. I really wish she wouldn't.

"No, like I literally can't even. When I found out that it was the unconventional challenge I panicked. But then I found these bags in the trash. I think they used to hold cookies or something. I did a hand treatment, designing my own pattern and painting them, and now you'd never know!" Michele is flitting about as she always does. Sometimes—frequently—her flitting makes me dizzy.

She's adjusting a seam on the back when her words finally register. "What do you mean unconventional challenge? Garbage? Bags?"

"You know, where we can't make your clothes from actual fabric. I raided the garbage outside a cookie factory and used the bags to make the material. That's what gives the skirt such movement."

And now the noise makes sense, except I don't know why there's an unconventional challenge. The show is finished. "Yes, but don't you think the sound is a bit ... conspicuous?" Inside my head, I want to rip the garment off and scrub down with bleach. I'm wearing garbage. Someday I'm going to be queen, and I'm dressed in refuse. Oh God, I may be sick.

I mean I may have grown up without a lot of worldly goods, but this is a new low. However, I don't have time to vomit or even bathe in hand sanitizer, as I'm being pushed through a dimly lit doorway. Outside, the press of people is tremendous. Perhaps even larger than outside the cathedral on our wedding day. The crowd leaves a berth around the red carpet, but nothing else separates me from them. Then suddenly, there's the hag from *The Princess Bride* yelling at me about how I had true love but threw it away. I try to protest that George was my love in the past, but he was no longer my true love. I don't know why I can hear the rustle of my gown over the cacophony of the crowd but I can. The crone continues to yell, calling me the "Queen of Garbage." The dress doesn't do much to contradict her. I again start to protest but she simply looks at me and meows.

I wake up with a start and stare into the celadon eyes of a large black-and-gray tiger cat chewing on the bag of oatmeal cookies I left on the end table.

I don't own a cat.

He (she?) doesn't seem to know that. He (she?) has made himself right at home, nonplussed by my presence. I wish I could say the same thing.

The cat takes one more bite of the bag, as if to prove that he can and then commences grooming, as if it's comfortable here. In my house.

I don't own a cat.

Just because I was thinking about it before I fell asleep doesn't mean it should happen. Slowly, I sit up on the couch, extracting myself from the yarn that has seemingly exploded all over. The cat pounces on the string, pushing the mass of yarn off the couch and across the floor. I'm mesmerized watching the display, partly because I'm discombobulated from my dream, but mostly because I don't own a cat.

Finally, the cat tires of the yarn and realizes it doesn't pose a threat. He lies down on top of the strands, and in a moment, falls asleep. I ask the cat where he came from, but he doesn't move. I wonder if cats dream. The question makes me think about my own dream.

I realize now that the rustling of my gown was actually the cat chewing on the bag. And *The Princess Bride* has always been a favorite here. Tomas loved it, although I don't always think he understood why it was funny when he would tell people, "Inconceivable." But I think the dream means more than just a fond reminiscing. I mean, it's pretty obvious that I don't think highly of myself for my actions with George.

Being back here, around him again, has made me relive it. That moment of teen angst and heartbreak that is so intense you're sure you're going to die.

And that's the other, not-so-subtle message from the dream. That I had true love. George. Yes, I gave it away.

That was fifteen years ago. I've married someone else. And that's going to be a difficult extraction. Never in a million years would I have thought Stephan would be Humperdink to my Buttercup. Without a doubt, I know he loves me. Well, loved me at least. Even with him putting the needs of the country first, I'm almost certain he doesn't plan to murder me and frame Guilder for it.

My heart hurts. Thinking of George makes it hurt. Thinking of Stephan makes it hurt. I tell this to the cat. He doesn't seem to care. I've decided to settle on him being a he. I inquire again where he came from, but he's close-lipped. Do cats have lips?

The cat refuses to answer my anatomy question as well. Seeing that I will get no answers from him, I decide to get something to eat in hopes it will help shake the unease created by the dream. The soup was hours ago, and I'm used to having elaborate meals every day.

Thanks to George, my fridge is fully stocked. I peruse the shelves and drawers, looking for something that will satisfy. I land on frozen pierogies. Gosh, I haven't had these—well, certainly not since Stephan and I were dating. I remember making them for him one time. It was all he could do not to laugh at me. Understandably, I was angry with him for his amusement at my simple food repertoire. What I don't understand is why Stephan didn't run for the hills then.

I almost wish he had. But he didn't. The poor man choked down my carbohydrate-and-fat-filled dinner as if it were chateaubriand. Later on that night, when I'd let my anger dissipate, I looked at Stephan. "Are you sure you don't want anything else to eat? I mean, something not from the freezer?"

He shook his head and pulled me in tight. "No, my dear. I'm full."

"How can you possibly be full still? I'm already hungry again, and your appetite is much more substantial than mine. There's no way my stupid pierogies will tide you over until morning."

"Darling, don't you understand? As long as I have you, my heart will be full. That's all that matters. I'll never need anything more than your love."

It's too bad that his idea of love didn't fall in line with loving me in his royal world. That the pressures and duty associated with being the crown prince were so much stronger than the love we shared. Part of me wonders if it would have been better never to have loved him. I'm not sure I buy the old adage that it's better to have loved and lost. Maybe, but it's certainly not better to have loved and been humiliated. And whether I want to admit it or not, this whole thing is downright humiliating.

While I'm in the fridge, getting out the butter, I see a bottle of cherry cola. I haven't had a soda in eons, as it's not a princessly beverage. George remembered that it was my favorite, and it dawns on me that the humiliation I'm feeling at the hands of

Stephan must be akin to what I put George through all those years ago.

They were right about karma.

So the best way to fix my life is to make it up to George. If I do that, maybe, just maybe, years down the road, when the dust has settled with the divorce and all, I'll be able to find the love I deserve.

Before I can come up with a solid plan (yes, I said a plan) to make it up to George, the door crashes open, causing me to jump out of my chair, knocking my soda over at the same time.

"Maryn! Oh Maryn! You're here! You're safe!"

I haven't heard Ma's voice so animated in years. The excited tone normally bothers Tomas, but I see he's not behind her. Perhaps he's still in the car.

I let the beverage spill onto the floor as I rush to hug my mother. Suddenly, in her arms, I'm six years old and seeking comfort because I broke my favorite record. Most of the other kids had cassettes, which we couldn't afford. It felt like that record was my only link to the outside world. Once again, that thread is tenuous and about to snap. It takes everything in my power not to let the tears gush forth. I have a feeling if I let them start I won't be able to stop them this time.

"Yes Ma, I'm here. Why are you here?" My voice is muffled against her shoulder as I bury my head into her. If I could crawl back in her womb, I probably would. At least I'd feel safe and wanted again. "Where's Tomas? Is he okay?" I look around her to see where he is, but he's nowhere to be seen.

"Tomas is with his care worker."

"Is he okay?"

"Yes, but that's my question to you. Stephan came to see me. He was frantic. He said you'd disappeared."

"Well, I left."

Ma pulls back, her cognac eyes filled with all the warmth I remember. "Does he know that?"

"Of course he does. I told him and his asshat father."

"You mean the *king*?"

"Same difference," I shrug.

Ma sets about cleaning up the mess on the table and floor while I stand there like a nincompoop. She doesn't say anything as she mops up. I know she's waiting for me to continue.

Deep in the recess of my brain, I know I should grab the rag from her hand and clean up my mess, but the past few years of living as royalty has dampened the part of my inner self that would never have dreamed of being waited on. Suddenly, I jolt into motion, grasping the cloth out of Ma's hand.

"It's my mess. I've got this." That was close. It was almost as if I were turning into one of *those* people. You know, the people who thought I was only good as a baby-making machine.

Ma stands there watching me clean. Once the mess has been taken care of, she sits at the table. I know I'm supposed to join her. She doesn't have to say a word. I don't want to fall apart again, but I know it's most likely inevitable.

"So, I left Stephan," I say coolly. I can do this. I can keep my composure.

"I gathered." Her voice is that calm, soothing voice that I'm used to, but the raised eyebrow tells me she is not pleased with me.

"I had to. I didn't have a choice."

"Do tell."

Wow. She is not pleased with me.

I launch in, telling her the gory details about my husband's illegitimate child, my father-in-law's hatred and disdain for me, and the plot to use my uterus for political gain. I finish and look at her, expecting the rush of sympathy.

It doesn't come.

"Well, it's not as if I could stay. Not with all that going on. They were even talking about taking me for insemination just to guarantee I'd be pregnant by election time!"

"I'm pretty sure that would be against the law."

"Not if you're the one making the law!" My voice is rising. Why doesn't she understand my side? Why is this even a question? I ask her as much.

Ma gets up and crosses the small kitchen to wash the dishes. I know she can't sit still. She always has to be busy. Hence the knitting. "When you agreed to marry Stephan, you knew what you were walking into. I asked if you were sure. You said you were willing to make whatever sacrifices you needed to be with him."

I remember those words, but somehow they don't seem applicable to this situation. "Ma, are you telling me that I should have stayed and been used as a pawn in the election?"

"No, I'm not saying that."

"It sounds like it." All my princess training has flown out the window and my emotion is written across my face and in the tone of my voice.

"Calm down. All I'm saying is that maybe you should have talked with Stephan about this before disappearing. He thinks you've been kidnapped."

"Well, that's stupid. I told him I was divorcing him. I packed my bags."

"Yes, but apparently no one saw you leave."

"How is that even possible? It seems they know my every movement. I had to get a car from the garage. Surely they can track it. I mean, if they can track my menstrual cycle they can find one of their own vehicles."

"I don't know, but I know someone's been sacked over it. Apparently, there was some implication that the head of the garage was in his cups."

"Ma, have you been reading my old romance novels again?"

"Anyway, no one was really sure why you left. They thought you may have been forced to stage it."

"And the big fight I had with the king and Stephan was part of it?"

"No, just unfortunate timing. You need to call him."

"I can't."

"Maryn." Her voice has taken on a stern tone I haven't heard since I was about eight. "Call him now. Let him know where you are and that you're alive and well."

"I can't. If I do, he'll send his royal henchmen to abscond with me." I look down at my feet, somewhat ashamed to admit the next part. "Plus, I did a factory reset on my phone and left it behind so he couldn't track me. I couldn't call him even if I wanted to."

Like a magician, Ma whips her phone out from I-don't-even-know-where and hands it to me. "Problem solved. He's in the contacts under SIL. Didn't want anyone who found my phone to be able to call him."

I have to laugh. "What, were you going to put it in under Prince Stephan?"

A blush darkens her cheeks, making her look a bit younger. "Maybe I did and maybe they made me change it."

"Who is they?" I ask, taking the phone from her hand. She turns back to the sink, cleaning it out even though it's already spotless.

"You're not the only one who had to go to Princess Academy. I had to go to Mother-in-Law School."

How had I not known this? I say as much.

"You were busy. But man, there are a lot of rules."

"Tell me about it."

"I don't need to. You learned what is right a long time before those stuffed shirts got a hold of you. Now call your husband and let him know you're alive and pissed."

Chapter 13

Sitting on my bed in my old room, holding my mother's phone in my hand, makes me feel like an insecure teenager all over again. What am I going to say to him? To go back to him would be admitting defeat. It would be selling myself. Selling myself short and into a life of virtual slavery. Sure, it would come with the finest crystal and pampering like I'd never imagined existed. But it would mean giving up everything I stand for.

But giving him up also means giving up everything I've ever wanted in life. To be loved. To be adored. To have security and safety. Heck, I'd even have armed guards. And staff.

I think I thought those things would make life easy. Or easier, at least. I didn't know what the cost of it all would be.

My happiness. My love.

Stephan's dancing blue eyes flash in my mind. God, I love those eyes—the mischievous twinkle when he's about to do something he knows he shouldn't. I will never again get to lose myself in those eyes while my body is pinned underneath him.

Cue the waterworks.

I can no longer see the phone to call Stephan, let alone the screen to dial him. I feel bad that he's upset, but he deserves it for breaking my heart by putting the whims of the monarchy before his concern for me.

The image of him on the television, distraught and weeping at my untimely demise, pops into my head. That thought causes me to sit straight up. Who am I kidding? I remember when his mother, Queen Margarethe, finally passed away after her long battle with cancer. He stood beside (and just a little behind) King Franklin, stone faced. I asked him about it one time. He told me that up to that point—and as far as I know, nothing's changed—he's never cried about his mother's death. It was, as he put it, "one of those things."

Losing me will undoubtedly be *one of those things* too.

So I need to stop shedding copious amounts of fluid over him. He needs to be *one of those things*.

I swallow several deep breaths, trying to pull myself together. I can do this. I don't even wait for him to speak.

"Stephan, it's me. I'm fine. I left. Not because someone forced me. Well, that's not true. You. You and your father forced me. I won't be changing my mind, so don't try. I don't need much from you, other than your support for Tomas and Ma. Don't punish them because I can't live how you want me to."

Without waiting for a reply, I disconnect the phone promptly. Perhaps I'm afraid that if he has a chance to speak my resolve will crumble. I don't know why the immediate ringing surprises me, but it causes me to drop the phone. Of course it's a palace number.

For some inexplicable—dumb—reason, I answer. It's his turn to rant.

"Maryn, please tell me where you are. I need to see you. I need to talk to you. I ... I can't let it end like this."

End like this. Not that he can't let it end, but he can't let it end like *this*. Meaning he needs me not to spill my guts to the country before the election, thereby ruining the monarchy's chance at winning. There will be no meeting. I can't bear to look at his stupid face.

"Yes, of course. I won't say anything to the press. I know that's what you're truly concerned about. That is where your true concern lies." I correct myself quickly. He hates when I end a sentence in a preposition. "You can release your official statement. I won't give any interviews. Just let me be."

The silence on the line hangs thick. "I see."

I know he's all stoic and crap from being born with a crown and scepter in his mouth, but I sort of expected more than "I see."

"Okay then. Well, I think that's about it." I have to end this now.

I'm about to disconnect when I hear Stephan's voice. "Maryn, wait!"

This is it—his impassioned plea for forgiveness. I will be strong and resist. Unless it's good enough and then I'll go running back with open arms.

"Please stay out of sight until an official statement is released. I'll send some security, but it will be low-key as not to garner attention."

A lot of words I've been instructed that a princess never uses run through my head. A string of curses that would make my plebian ancestors proud. Instead of letting them fly, I scream into the pillow.

After a few minutes I head back down to the kitchen, slowly sliding Ma's phone across the table to her. "It's over."

Her eyes look as broken as they did the day my father left with Mrs. Panagogus. I didn't think I could feel any worse than I already did. I let her down. I failed at being a wife on the most basic level. Not to mention by failure to rule—or at least represent—the country.

"Ma, I'm so sorry. Don't worry. You and Tomas will be taken care of. Nothing will change. You will get to keep the apartment and the services and everything. I can't ask you to go back because I'm not strong enough to handle this."

She doesn't say anything but instead takes me in her arms and holds me through another round of tears. Finally she pulls back and wipes my cheeks, much like she did when I was a child. "I give you one more day to weep and wallow, and then you have to get up and get going."

"Going? I'm not going anywhere. I can't, not really. I at least need to stay hidden until the election is over. It wouldn't surprise me if they keep the divorce a secret until then."

"Then you can't really leave the house even, can you? What will you do?"

"I started knitting again." That reminds me about my weird dream and the cat, so I tell Ma about it all.

"Oh, that's George's cat. He comes over here all the time."

"But how does he get in? I woke up and he was there, eating the cookie bag."

"We keep the basement window open a crack for him. Tomas loves Inigo."

"Inigo? As in Inigo Montoya?"

"Yes. George let Tomas name him and that's what he picked. Mostly because the father cat was left on the doorstep dead, so Tomas thought this cat would be looking for who killed his father."

The connections to the movie *The Princess Bride* sends shivers down my spine. I'm also trying to ignore the memory that it was during this movie that George kissed me for the first time.

Darkness has settled in, and I beg Ma to stay the night even though I know she won't. Can't. She's got to get back to Tomas. I understand. I've always understood. But it doesn't make it any easier to be alone right now.

Regardless, I am alone if you don't count Inigo who is now meowing at me. I imagine he's demanding some food or something. I'd shoo him outside to catch a mouse or something, but I don't want to lose the company of another living creature.

The pain surrounding my heart feels as real as a heart attack. Perhaps I'm dying. That would serve Stephan right. There's no way they'd be able to spin it in the media—me dying of a broken heart.

I can't stay within these walls one more moment. It's the same feeling that inspired me to flee the palace in the first place. Once outside it's different. The night sky, cool with the fall temperature, makes me feel calm. Inky swirls of purple and navy thread through the black, and the stars light up the sky.

I'd forgotten about the stars. It's been so long since I've seen them. In the capital city the lights drown out the glow of the stars. As kids, George and I used to sleep out in the field from June through August. The last summer, before the end, we shared a blanket, awaking each morning tangled in each other. Despite the chill and the sense of loneliness, I want nothing more than to go out there for the night. Perhaps, I reason, I'll feel the sense of contentment I felt that summer fifteen years ago.

Or not. Good God, it's freezing out here. I don't get this autumnal weather. Two days ago I was melting in a puddle of my own perspiration while I was stranded on the side of the road. Tonight I may die of hypothermia. This stupid knitted blanket with all the holes in it is doing nothing to keep me warm. That's enough of this magical, soul-searching experience for me. I'll have to find myself elsewhere.

The morning, although it brings a slight warm up, brings no more clarity to my situation. My marching orders from Stephan, *His Royal Assness*, are to lay low. Keep out of public sight for a while. I don't even have to ask how long because I know. This bloody election has ruined everything.

Stephan's inability to stand up to his father has ruined everything.

Stephan's prioritizing Montabago over me has ruined everything.

It's not enough that my father chose someone else over his own family. Now I marry a man who does the same thing. My father denied Tomas much like Stephan is denying Artem. And all for what? Is my father happy with his decisions? Have the last fifteen years been good to him? Does he ever look back and find himself filled with regret and remorse?

I've never wanted to know the answer to these questions. For me, it was easier to simply *not think* about it. Not talk about him. Never let him into my life again.

But now I need to know.

Even if I wanted to ask my father directly—which I'm not ready to do—I wouldn't know where to find him. Oh sure, the media dug him up for a few salacious stories when Stephan and I were first engaged. It was the one time in my life I appreciated the media ban within the palace.

Before I'm even aware of what I'm doing, my legs are striding in the general direction of my next-door neighbor's house. Without knocking, without waiting to be invited in, I swing open the screen door, letting the faded wood bang against the side of the house as I march through.

"I'm ready to talk about it."

Chapter 14

"No."

George's answer is not what I'm expecting to hear. It shouldn't shock me, but for some reason it does.

"No, George. I need some answers."

"No." He's busy slamming things around, obviously looking for something. He's dressed in faded jeans that are probably old enough to drive, as well as a flannel shirt. I can see the banded collar of a Henley just below his neck. He finally picks up a belt, which was hanging on a hook by the door, and threads it around his narrow waist.

"You can't tell me no."

"Um, I believe I just did. Now if you'll be so kind, get out."

In theory—okay, in reality—I deserve this treatment. I did tell him, whilst I was stamping on his heart, that I would *never* want to discuss it with him. And by *it*, of course, I mean the torrid and sordid affair between our parents. It's not as if I was grossed out by the whole George being my stepbrother thing. I never got far enough—not until many years and lots of bottles of wine later—to even approach processing that ick factor.

I trail after George as he heads into the mudroom and pulls on his dirty, worn work boots. I look around. Everything about the Panagogus place is worn and faded. There's nothing *new* at all. In fact, there are many things that are old and patched together. It makes me wonder about their financial state. Mr. Panagogus was a farmer, but everyone knows that it's hard to make a living at that. Mrs. Panagogus was a lawyer working in the same firm as my father. They used to ride to work together. I stop that line of thought before it can lead to images of them and riding. Yuck.

Once she left I doubt she sent money back for George. We all know my father didn't provide any financial support. I wonder if they've been living hand-to-mouth since then. It certainly would explain a lot. Now I have to know if George and his father are okay. I need them to be. The thought that I left without regard for their well-being—even though it's *exactly* what I did— fills me with guilt. The sound of the screen door slamming brings me back to attention.

"George, wait! Where are you going?"

He stops for a moment. "Are you really doing this?" Without waiting for an answer, George stalks off across the yard to the barn.

"Doing what?" I say, breathless. He walks fast. I don't remember his gait being that quick. On the other hand, he was never trying to get away from me before.

"Coming back, barging into my house. Dredging up the past which you had *forbade* me to ever talk about. Following me around and being generally annoying. Don't you have a tiara to polish or something?"

The bitter bite to his voice takes me aback. "If I had anything else to be doing or anywhere else to be, I'd go. As it is, I'm under orders to stay put and out of sight."

George grunts and continues walking. I wait a beat and then follow him, struggling to keep up. Dang, I'm out of shape.

He disappears inside the barn, and a moment later the roaring of a large engine startles me. George comes riding out on a large tractor that has certainly seen better days, puffing clouds of black exhaust. Large noise-dampening headphones surround his ears, and he makes it a point not to look at me as he drives past. Before I can even figure out what I'm doing, I lunge for the tractor, attempting to jump on. In my head I can see the perfect execution. With the grace and choreography of a ballet dancer, I leap onto the footboard, swing my opposite leg over, and slide gracefully into the seat behind George.

We all know my life does not go that way. Instead I trip and fall flat on my face. George doesn't even see what I've attempted to do (thank goodness for small favors) and keeps puttering on, leaving me choking and sputtering in the dust, my hands and knees scraped and bleeding.

Fantastic.

Sitting in the dirt, I try to evaluate the situation. What did I think I was doing anyway? Why did I think leaping onto the tractor was going to help things? George obviously doesn't want to talk to me. I should be grateful for the assistance he's provided and not ask any more of him. He's not part of my life. I made sure of that a long time ago. I need to accept the bed I made.

Which now will include neither George nor Stephan.

Not that I'm thinking about sex, because that's the furthest thing from my mind. Except now that I'm trying to not think about it, it's all I can think about.

I'm never going to have sex again. Who's going to want me? I mean other than the total creepers who'd get their rocks off being involved with someone who used to be famous for a little bit.

I'm screwed. Or not, as the case may be.

I know I should pull myself up by the proverbial boot strap and mog on, but I can't seem to motivate myself. So it's here I lie in the dust and dirt. I know eventually I'll need to get up, but Ma has allowed me this one last day to wallow, and damn if I'm going to let it go to waste.

After all, I'm the Queen of Wallowing.

I'm so good at it that I don't notice the feet at first. Not until the voice attached asks, "And what in hell do you think you're doing here?" American. Definitely American. Fantastic. Then I take stock. Shabby-chic brown work boots that lead up to legs clad in skin-tight denim. A flannel shirt buttoned over a snug camisole, which reveals a well-developed bosom. And an honest-to-God cowboy hat. She looks as if she belongs on the cover of a cowboy romance novel. "I'm asking you, what do you think you're doing here?"

Hastily I stand up, trying to brush the dirt off me, to no avail. "I'm, uh, well, I'm ..."

"Oh for Pete's sake, stop stammering and spit it out."

Her abruptness, coated with that Southern twang, takes me aback.

"I'm wallowing."

"This here is private property, so you best be wallowing somewhere else."

"It's okay. I know the owner. He doesn't mind me being here." I try to brush the dirt off again, but it's not helping.

"I mind. I will call the police."

At least some of my princess training kicks in, because something makes me hold back from reading this cowpoke the riot act. Instead of saying what I really want to say, I gently hold up my hands. "No need for that. I'll catch up with George later."

It's then that I see Miss Kitty here has a shotgun (or rifle—I honestly don't know the difference) partially hidden behind her back. "Good Lord, what were you planning on doing with *that*?" I point to the weapon.

"We take our no trespassing seriously. And sometimes the police around here are slow. So if you'll kindly leave, I won't have to put a bullet where the sun don't shine."

This is not an expression with which I'm familiar, but I'm guessing wherever that is, it wouldn't be pleasant.

"Who put you in charge?" I can't stop myself from challenging this pushy American, gun or no gun.

"I'm in charge of security here. Plus I'm engaged to the owner."

"Since when do they have security here?" I look her up and down. She's had some work done if her bloated lips are any indication. Her hair is the unnatural white-blond that a bottle of bleach provides, and it tumbles in stiff curls over her shoulders. "And aren't you a bit on the young side for Mr. Panagogus?" Part of me wants to high five the man for finding a young chippy, but most of me is grossed out.

"George is only five years older than I am, not that it's any of your business." She's adopted a wide stance. Probably a good thing because I'm almost sure she has a thigh gap and a perfect ass, and there's no way I can handle that and the fact that she's engaged to George.

My George.

I have no right to call him that, I know. That mere fact doesn't stop the thought from running through my head.

"Are you going to tell me what you're doing here?" She raises her eyebrow.

"I, uh, was over here talking to George."

She glances around. "I don't see him anywhere. Anyway, why were you on the ground?"

"He took the tractor out to the fields, and I, uh, felt light headed and needed to lie down." This is probably more plausible than my failed attempt at being a stuntwoman. "Do you mind putting the gun away? It makes me nervous."

"Oh, sorry." She looks down at the gun. "Can't be too careful these days. You know, ever since—" She nods in the general direction of my house. "Well, things have been crazy here for George since the press found out where *she* grew up."

If I didn't know better, I would think Annie Oakley here doesn't know who I am. I mean, she knows who Princess Maryn is, obviously, but not that she's me. Or I'm her. Or whatever.

"She?"

"The princess." The spite in her voice is unmistakable. "Ever since the tart decided to shack up with the crown prince, George's life has been a living hell. There's invasion of privacy on a daily basis. And then the prying into George's life. He's a very private person, you know, and because he and the princess used to date, the press hounded him relentlessly. It was just like Diana."

In the back of my head, I'm thinking that if George were such a private person, which, in fact he is, he probably wouldn't appreciate these details being shared with a stranger. For all she knows, I could be a reporter or paparazzi.

"The press wanted to catch George moping around after she got engaged, but he wouldn't let them see him like that. Even when the bitch sent him an invitation to the wedding. I mean, who does that? Invite your ex-boyfriend to your wedding. I hope they're making her life miserable in that palace because it's what she deserves."

Well, it's pretty clear she has no idea who I am. I guess it's a good sign that I can fly under the radar. On the other hand, with the way she's going off about me, I have such a desire to set her straight. But still, it's interesting to know what she—and George—think of me.

None of it's good.

Chapter 15

This is perhaps one of the most peculiar situations I've ever had the fortune—or misfortune—in which to find myself. I'm sitting in George's kitchen, a room I've been in thousands of times in my life, being shown around by a stranger, as if I'm a stranger.

This buxom blond, Dina Marie, is engaged to my former love.

And she hates my guts with the heat of a thousand suns.

Honestly, it's like something from a bad TV show. My dream with the garbage dress and *The Princess Bride* somehow seems less surreal than this very moment.

The best—worst—weirdest—part is that she has no idea who I am. I mean she knows Princess Maryn. Knows and apparently has strong opinions about. But she has no inkling that I'm her. Or she's me. Or whatever. That we're one and the same. I know I should say something, but I can't seem to. Like watching a car accident about to happen and being frozen in place.

"And then she goes on TV and smiles down on the designers as if they're the poor peasants. Does she not remember where she came from? I've been to her house, and let me tell you, it's a far cry from the palace."

Any amusement I'd anticipated in giving Dina Marie enough rope to hang herself then embarrassing the heck out of her has evaporated into thin air. Her comments are the exact reason I stopped using the internet. Stephan could do it, but I never could after we became a public entity. I couldn't handle the scrutiny, no matter how true or false the claims. It didn't matter if they said I was pregnant by Freddie Mercury. It would still hurt. The only way to feel okay about myself was to avoid it at all costs. And now here it is being thrown in my face.

"Maybe the princess was nervous about being on camera, so she didn't come across that great. I've heard being relaxed in that setting can be difficult."

"No, she's a stuck-up bitch. You can tell. Plus, I know for a fact she is. She was like that even before she got herself in with the prince and on TV."

That one smarts a bit.

Well, a lot.

Because if she thinks I was always a stuck-up bitch, it must be because George told her so. I use all of my princess training (who ever thought it'd come in so handy?) and say, "Oh? Is that right?"

Dina Marie takes the bait. "Oh, yes. George won't say so directly, but people in town who knew her say she was—I don't know how you put it over here, but back home we'd call her white trash. Is that a thing here?"

"No, I don't believe I've ever heard that before." Poor, certainly. Unfortunate, most definitely. But no one's ever called me trash to my face, other than the old lady in my dream.

"Well, you know, she doesn't come from good stock. Her father was a good-for-nothing womanizer. He stole George's mom!" Dina Marie's hands are waving wildly about, and she makes it sound like Mrs. Panagogus was a painting that my dad swiped in the middle of the night. "And then, she's got a *special* brother who she's had sent away so he's not out in public. And her mother has to go with the brother. The impression I get is that she's ashamed of them."

Sent away! Ashamed! I can feel the color flooding my cheeks. No one talks about Ma and Tomas that way.

"Dina, that's enough." The deep timbre of George's voice is enough to startle both of us. I wonder if Dina Marie knows him well enough to know that this is his really-ticked-off face? George turns that harsh gaze to me. "What are you still doing here?"

"I fell in the yard after you left. Dina Marie was nice enough to help me up."

The only response from George is a raised eyebrow. He knows there's more to the story than that, without me even saying it.

"That's right. She doesn't look like a snooping press person. But I never did catch your name, sugar?"

I look from her to George and can't help but roll my eyes at him. I think he overheard enough to know what's coming, as he shakes his head slightly in response.

"Dina, this is Maryn. I mean, Her Royal Highness—"

"George, stop. You don't need to call me that. In fact, especially in lieu of the current situation, I'd prefer it if you didn't." I stand, preparing to exit.

Dina's mouth plops open and hangs there, which is not an attractive look for her, or anyone else for that matter.

"I'll walk you home."

Well, that causes Dina Marie's mouth to snap shut instantaneously. She looks from me to George and back to me, her eyes narrowing. I don't think she's a fan of mine.

I head to the door. "Goodbye, Dina Marie. It was, ah, interesting."

I half expect George to go and soothe his now-seething fiancée, but he joins me right away. I feel the need to fill the silence between the two of us, but I'm not even sure how to begin. Finally, after about ten minutes, I start. "Well, I guess I know where we stand, based on what Dina told me about ... me." It's probably one of the oddest sentences I've ever said.

"You don't know anything."

I'm sure George is talking about Dina, but that statement applies to most of my life at the moment. "You're right. Absolutely right. But Dina Marie had to get her information from somewhere. And if not her fiance, then where?"

"From people in town. You know, the small-minded, large-mouthed people you've always detested. It's not as if they changed just because you became the princess. If anything, I think they got worse."

"So you don't hate me?" I don't know why this matters so much to me, but in this moment it does. I think I'll survive the end of my marriage, but I don't know if I can handle hearing that George hates me.

"You know I never could."

George's soft-spoken words break something inside of me. How have I gotten it so wrong? How have I messed up my life so completely and totally? The words are still hanging thick between us when I say the very next thing that pops into my head.

"You're getting married."

"It's the natural thing to do." George's words are so matter of fact. I can't help but wonder if I irreparably damaged him.

"Right. Of course."

"You got married."

"Yes, well, we see how well that turned out." We've reached my back door by now. "George?" I turn to face him and really look at him for the first time.

"Yes?"

Gazing into his green eyes, I feel the years—the history—melting away. I need to focus to remember what I want to say. "When you marry, make sure it's for the right reasons. Don't lie—to yourself or to her—about why you want to get married. Please?"

"Did he lie to you?" It's not the answer I expected.

"Yes. He lied about loving me. Well not lied, but he loved his country more than me. And he used me as a pawn in his game with his father. The only love in Stephan's life is his country. I don't know how I could have been so stupid as to not see it."

"It looks like he's in love with you."

"He's a good actor."

"Maybe so. It looked like you two were in love."

"One of us was."

"It's a terrible thing when a relationship is one-sided." George regards me for a moment before dropping his gaze to the ground. "I should be getting back to Dina. I've likely some explaining to do."

He turns without looking at me again. "George?" I call, almost desperately. It's enough to halt his steps but not to bring him around to face me.

"So you don't hate me?"

I see his shoulders drop. Softly he mutters, "Don't you know I never could?"

Chapter 16

"George, wait!" I hate the desperation in my voice, but I can't hold it in any longer. "Please stay and talk to me."

That stops him. It feels like eons before he turns around. "I don't know what else you have to say. You've already said *all the words*."

It tugs my heart to remember how George and I used to talk all night. One night I told him I was afraid one day I'd use up all the words, and I'd have nothing left to say.

"No, I have more to say. I have more you need to hear."

Without looking at me, George returns to the house. He walks through the kitchen and into the living room. He takes up the spot on the couch where he'd spent years. He's more at home here than I am. Before I know it, the cat has materialized out of thin air, curling up next to George.

It's as if they belong here.

I'm the only one who doesn't. Or do I?

The words are swirling and screaming through my head, all demanding to be spoken at once. I don't even know where to start. So that's what I say. "I'm not sure how to begin. I don't know where the beginning is. I ..." I falter.

"What happened with ... *him*?"

"I made a terrible mistake." I can't look at George while I say this.

"You got caught up in the excitement, didn't you? You always loved your stories. Those damn romance novels where the handsome prince swoops in and saves the damsel in distress. How long did it take you to realize that you need some substance?"

I do not like George's tone. Not at all. If I didn't know better, I'd think he sounded, well, jealous. But that can't be. George and I were long over before I even met Stephan. And besides, he's engaged to Dina Marie.

"My mistake is not that I married him. I mean, well, it is, but that's not what I mean."

"What do you mean then?"

"I was ... foolish. Stupid, even, to think that it was true and real. It wasn't. It was all a show."

"What was a show? The show? Of course it was a show." George gets up and stalks off to the kitchen. A moment later he yells, "You don't even have any beer here."

"Of course not. There wasn't any food here. You bought pretty much everything here. If you didn't buy beer, then there's none here."

He rummages for a few more minutes, opening and closing cabinets. I hear the distinct clinking of glasses and ice cubes. George returns, putting a tumbler down in front of me and downing most of the contents of the one in his hand. I raise my eyebrow.

"Isn't it a bit early in the day for the hard stuff?"

"It's going to make this much better."

One of the first rules of Princess Academy is that I can't really drink. Oh sure, a sip here and there to be polite, but intoxication, even in private, is a big NO, with a capital N-O. The glass sits there, taunting me.

To hell with the palace. I grab the tumbler and toss it back.

Big mistake. I don't drink anymore. And when I do, I don't drink liquid death. It's probably whiskey of some sort, but it's more of what I imagine engine fluid tasting like. The coughing and choking that ensues is the antithesis of ladylike.

Screw ladylike.

"I'll take another."

"Yes, Your Highness." George does a mock bow. I don't know if it's the title or tone of his voice that bothers me more.

"Don't call me that. Ever."

It hits me. I'll never be called Your Highness again. For a poor girl from the wrong side of the tracks, that was a sweet perk. I used to fold other people's underwear and cook food for them. I'll probably have to go back to something like that again. It's not as if I have other skills to support myself. Where is George with that drink?

This time he brings the bottle out with him. Probably a good thing.

I take a slow sip to avoid choking and try to start again. "It's the election."

"What does the election have to do with your marriage?" George frowns. It was the face he used to make when trying to do algebra.

"Everything."

"Maybe I should cut you off."

"You're the one who encouraged me to drink in the first place."

"That was before I realized you were an instant drunk. Just add liquor."

I laugh and it comes out as a hiccough. "I should get that on a shirt or sign or something."

"So what is this about the election?"

"It's why we got married." My response is again met with that confused look. I sigh. I can't believe I have to explain this all out. Granted, I didn't see it myself, but now it's as clear as the sun in the sky.

"Stephan was required to get married to produce an heir. He thought the best way to stick it to his father was to marry the opposite of expectations. In other words, me."

The words seem even worse now that I've said them aloud. I imagine them hanging in the air like a cloud of poison.

"I think Stephan envisioned using me and my background to gain support. I fit right in. It couldn't have worked any better. Not only did he pluck me out of the dregs of the workforce, but I was deserted by my father and have a disabled brother. It was like the trifecta of pity."

George's frown deepens. "He was using you?"

"It looks that way. As much as my father is absent, and always has been, Stephan's is overbearing and controlling. I guess we both have daddy-issues."

That realization is profound, but it doesn't really help the situation. Stephan would have to see it as well. And even if he did, it wouldn't change the fact that he doesn't feel about me the way I feel about him. Felt about him. I correct myself. I can't let myself love him like that anymore. I can shut it off, just like I did with George. I'm good at that.

Except now I look at George and things start to swim. Maybe it's the whiskey. Yeah, I'm sure that's it. "I'm such a mess."

"Yes, you are. Do you even know what you want?"

That question is impossible to answer, because all the things I want are impossible. I want Stephan to not be the crown prince. I want my dad to have loved me. I want not to have broken George. I want my life to be the perfect fairy tale instead of this big heated mess.

"I guess I just want to go back to normal."

"Normal? What's that?" I don't have to look at George to know he's rolling his eyes.

I shrug. "I don't know. Maybe not normal but easy. Well, easier. Certainly not this hard."

"I don't understand what's so hard about your life. You don't have to work. You're spoiled rotten. You have no cares, no worries. Why can't you be content with that?"

George's words are a slap in the face, and not even the whiskey can soften the blow.

"Yes, well I'm sure that's how you see it. I'm sure that's how everyone sees it. Just because you don't perceive my problems as important as yours doesn't mean they don't matter."

"Seriously, what problems? Are you struggling to make ends meet? Working your land 24-7 to pay the bills? Worrying every season that if the weather doesn't cooperate, you might lose it all? Letting the tax bill sit there because you know you can't afford to pay it? Taking care of the property next door out of some misguided sense of loyalty that has never ever been reciprocated? Had your father move away because he couldn't handle the attention and invasion of privacy from a mess someone else created?"

George's problems are real. I certainly remember those days of living paycheck to paycheck and still not having enough. But I don't like his tone.

"You're blaming me for everything?" I jump to my feet. "How is this all my fault?"

"Do you know how hard it is to work the land? Now I have to do it without my dad since he moved. He couldn't handle the stress of the trespassers and the constant media presence. He was on the verge of having a breakdown."

"Your dad moved?"

"That's what you get out of this? Yes, my dad left. Just like yours. Are you happy now? I don't have either parent because of you."

His words knock me down. Like literally. My knees buckle and I sink to the couch. I've ruined his life. I know tears are streaming down my cheeks, and there's nothing I can do to stop them.

George kneels down in front of me. "And the most messed up part?"

I can't imagine what's more messed up than him blaming me for this situation, although I don't deny I brought about the press business.

"I don't care. I'd go through everything all over again. I'd walk on hot coals every single day."

I have no idea what he's talking about. "What? Why?" My words croak out, barely above a whisper.

He leans in, his face inches from mine. "For you. I do it all for you."

Oh. My. Gosh.

I need to borrow a line from Michele. I can't even.

Because then George's lips are on mine. Hot. Demanding. Punishing. Loving. His body presses into me, and I succumb to it, lying back onto the couch, his weight on top of me.

George is kissing me. He's *kissing* me. Kissing *me*. It's warm and comfortable and ... completely wrong. I should not be doing this. Not at all. My loins finally cede control to my brain and I'm able to push George off.

"Stop, please."

George lifts up, his eyes scanning my face. "I'm not sorry. You ..." He sinks back to the opposite side of the couch. "I ... probably shouldn't have done that."

"No, I'm married." As if that's the only reason.

"But you won't be for long, will you?" George looks hopeful.

It looks as if I've got even more to think about now.

Great.

Chapter 17

It never occurred to me when I was little to want more than George. That there would be more than our lives, working together, and being a happy family.

I shunned that dream when I was sixteen.

And now, here it was being presented to me. Offered again, as if the past fifteen years hadn't happened. Like I hadn't ignored him all this time. Like I hadn't married someone else. Like he wasn't engaged to someone else.

"What about ... everything?" I don't need to specify. George knows what I'm thinking. He's always known.

"I expect it'll be messy for a while. We'd probably have to be rather discreet."

"George! You can't possibly be talking about this now. I've only left my husband three days ago. It's not even public yet. And you're *still* engaged!"

"I don't have to be. I'll go break it off right now."

I can't believe the coldness of his attitude toward Dina Marie. I mean, it's not as if she's the president of my fan club or anything, but she doesn't deserve this either. I stand up from the couch. "I think maybe you should go now."

"You're the one who asked me to stay."

"I didn't ask you to kiss me."

He looks at me for a beat. "I was so angry with you for so long. I didn't know how you could blame *me* for what *they* did. Just as I finally thought I was getting over you, you started dating him. It turned everything here upside down. Your mom and Tomas were completely overwhelmed. My father couldn't sleep for fear of people sneaking onto the property. He nearly went mad. He started having health problems. Dina actually came here to help with security."

"She had a shotgun or rifle or something."

"She knows how to use it." His face wears a look of pride.

"You don't want to hurt her."

"No, she's fantastic. Absolutely smashing."

I want to ask if he loves her, but I don't want to hear that answer. If he does, it will probably kill me. If he doesn't, then it puts the whole matter in my hands and begs a question I'm not prepared to answer.

I can't look away from George, but I know if he holds my gaze any longer, I may not be able to resist him.

What the heck is wrong with me? I shouldn't be thinking about this. I can't be thinking about this. My life is in shambles. This would only make things a bazillion times more complicated.

I inch closer to George. My hand sneaks out, reaching for his, our fingers just brushing. His hands are rough from work, so different from Stephan's manicured digits. I look at George. Everything is so familiar yet so different at the same time. Like that scar on his eyebrow. I reach up and touch it. "Where'd this come from?"

His hand closes over mine, still on his eyebrow, causing me to cup the side of his face in my palm.

"I wish I could say it was something that would impress you. I don't know that I'll ever be able to impress you again. But please give me the chance to try."

Words are not forming in my brain. It's too chaotic in there with the crush of emotions that's been building for days. But then the crashing in my brain is replaced by a loud thudding at the front door. I pull my hand back as if it's on fire, the spell broken.

The pounding continues and I jump to my feet, prepared to answer the door. George pulls my arm, halting any progress. "Stop. You can't answer that."

"Of course I can. There's someone at my door."

Bang. Bang. Bang.

"Yes, but who? Are you prepared for who or what may be on the other side? What if it's a crazy stalker? What if it's the paparazzi?" That damn eyebrow raises again. "What will you say if you pull open the door to the snap of camera flashes?"

I hate those damn flashes. I'm not the most photogenic person in the world, and I know they'd have a field day with how I look now.

"Your Highness?" Bang. Bang. Bang. "Are you in there? Please answer the door."

Sigh.

I break free from George and move to open the door. Relief washes over Daniel's face. "Oh, Your Highness. You're all right."

I step aside, indicating Daniel should enter. A smile spreads across his face and then freezes the moment he sees George. Daniel's back stiffens. A quick glance indicates a similar defensive pose from George.

"George, this is Daniel Von Windringham." I'm glad I catch myself before calling him Von Windbag. "He's Stephan's right hand. And probably the left. Daniel, this is George. He's—"

"I'm quite aware of who Mr. Panagogus is. I certainly didn't expect to find him here though." Daniel's tone is cold and dismissive, not at all the jovial jokester he often was with Stephan.

"Yes, well, George and I haven't seen each other in a number of years, as I'm sure you are aware." I can't help the bite in my voice. Of course he's aware. They seem to know everything I do. No doubt that's why Daniel showed up the moment George and I were alone together.

"If Mr. Panagogus would kindly leave, we have some important business to discuss." There was no mistaking the tone, which frankly said, "Get out. Now."

George looks from Daniel to me and back to Daniel. "I'm sorry, chap. Can't do that. Maryn and I were in the middle of an important discussion ourselves."

Say what? Nope. A whole lotta nope. No way is George going to bully me like this too.

"George, I think I'm okay. Plus, I really can't continue on with our conversation until other things are resolved, now can I?"

George growls. Legit *growls* his response. "Fine. You know where to find me."

I am so irritated by everything in this moment that I don't bother checking my response before it flies out of my mouth. "Yes, I know where to find you. With your *fiancée.*"

I don't know why I have to throw that in there. I'm not jealous. Okay, maybe I am. Just a little. George is mine. I had him first. I neglect to think about the fact that I moved on.

This is probably not my finest moment.

Once George leaves through the back door, indicating just how familiar he is with the place, I motion for Daniel to come and sit in the living room. I see his eyes roving, taking in all the details of my childhood home.

"So, well, this is where I come from. From where I come. From whence I came. Crap, I don't know. This is where I live."

Daniel smiles at my attempt to speak Princess-ease.

"You can see why I was never cut out for it, right? I mean, this is home. Stephan certainly did an adequate job of scraping the bottom of the barrel when finding me."

"We can't help who our parents are or to what station we are born. You should realize that more than anyone. And that it goes both ways."

I wrinkle my brow. "What do you mean by that?"

"Stephan can't help being born a prince any more than you could help being born here. You can't hold it against him."

"That's true." I pick up my glass and take one last small sip. There's more in the tumbler, but the whiskey is making my stomach twist and turn. Great.

Lactose and alcohol intolerant. What's next, gluten? I say a quick mental prayer to the gods of wheat that it won't come to fruition and put my glass back down. "What I can hold against Stephan is his deception and how he used me."

"He's never used you."

"That's bull and you know it. He only married me, A. because he was told to, and B. to get back at his father for making him get married. I'm sure Stephan would have rather spent the majority of his life partying and sowing his wild oats with the likes of Dominicka."

"You know that's not true and not fair, Your Highness."

"You can quit it with the 'Your Highness.' I want this divorce fast-tracked and for you all to leave me alone."

A look of pain shoots across Daniel's face. "You don't mean that."

"Oh, don't I? You know, I can see King Franklin and your father coming up with this stupid, antiquated farce. They are so out of touch that I can see them thinking that a royal baby would be enough to secure the monarchy for the next hundred years. But I thought Stephan was smarter than that. I would have thought you'd know better as well."

"That's not why Stephan married you. He married you because he loves you."

"How would you know? It's not as if you were there. Or were you? Listening. Watching. Taking notes." Suddenly I've a mental image of Daniel in the bushes outside Stephan's dorm suites at University, wearing big earphones attached to an antenna, trying to overhear our conversations.

"No, you know I wasn't around. Stephan insisted I come back to help with this. With you."

"Locking me in the tower wasn't a sufficient enough strategy?"

"What are you talking about?" His face is growing red.

I must be rattling Daniel. He just ended his sentence in a preposition. That's a demerit. "You know."

"I don't." His face flushes a shade darker.

"You're a terrible liar, but I'll use it to my advantage. What I mean, *as if you don't already know*, is that they're keeping me in the palace. I get to attend boring things, but only if the entire royal family is there. You know, to babysit me. I've asked to go to charity things and get involved and perhaps help people. I keep getting told that because of the election, I'm not allowed. That it'd be seen as trying to buy votes. But we know that's not true, now is it?"

Daniel's mouth opens, then closes.

"Don't lie to me, Daniel. For the love of God, show some respect. A modicum of courtesy, please. Be honest."

His shoulders sag a bit. "It wasn't Steph's idea."

"No, of course not. But nothing ever is, is it?"

"What do you mean by that?"

"He's a good boy who does whatever Daddy tells him to."

"In this case, yes. King Franklin wanted to limit your public exposure."

"Because he's embarrassed by me, right?"

"No, but the answer is embarrassing."

I raise my eyebrow. "Do tell."

Daniel stands and begins pacing. "King Franklin thought that if you were not too tired from working too much, you'd get pregnant sooner."

"Does he know I'm on birth control? I mean, he seems to know everything else about me."

"Apparently, Stephan has been rather elusive about whether you two are actually trying."

"Good God. I'm surprised he's not collecting our sheets to look for proof of consummation of our marriage and my menstrual cycle." I do read a lot of romance novels. That was a common maneuver way back when. You know, when King Franklin was young.

"He thought if you were home and bored, you'd start to think having a baby would be a good way to spend your time."

I cannot believe that man.

"So he really thinks a baby would win the election for him? Why not bring Artem in then? The public would go crazy, especially if the palace welcomed him in. I mean, Stephan and the king were blindsided by it. They were the victims. It could be huge for them. I don't understand why they—you—don't focus on that."

Daniel picks up the bottle of whiskey from the coffee table and takes a drink. A long one.

"I know why Stephan loves you. You're a good person, and you only see the good in people. Maybe you're right to get out now. I know I'm here to make you come home, but maybe I shouldn't. You might be better off. I think you most likely will be. You don't need this one true love. You'll find someone else to love. To love you. With whom to have that family. Maybe George. But not Stephan."

His sudden about-face has me confused. Is he trying reverse psychology on me?

"Stephan won't ever love anyone the way he loves you. He *changed* for you. But you're right. You can't change the fact that he does what he's told. And always will. You'll always be second. And Maryn, you deserve to be first."

Chapter 18

A week goes by. Then two. I putter around the house, cleaning stem to stern. I've made great progress on knitting a blanket, after ripping it out and starting over only three times. Okay, four times. It's a beautiful white yarn that's so soft, it feels as if it's made from the clouds. I don't know why I'm making this blanket or what I'll do with it when it's done. Perhaps I'll try to sell my knitting projects at a local shop. I bet something handcrafted by the former Princess of Montabago would fetch some nice coin.

I try not to watch TV. I really do. The election coverage is dominating everything. It's either our election or the one in America, which is, frankly, embarrassing. I no longer miss my phone. Well, that's mostly because Ma got me a TracFone so we can be in touch and text and whatnot. But I don't miss going online, not that I did that much before. She's also brought me money so I can have food.

Yup. Still relying on my mother to take care of me.

I wish she could be here. She's been stalling Tomas about visiting home again. My being here would be too confusing for him. Plus it's still a big hush-hush thing, and the world does not seem to know that I've left Stephan. There's been a little speculation about my absence from the world stage, but the current buzz is that I'm either in ill health or pregnant. Okay, I still see a little on TV.

It wouldn't surprise me if the palace released that last rumor.

The brief coverage I've seen suggests that the Salzach Monarchy will no longer be ruling in about six weeks. Nine if you count the time needed to elect a parliament. I wonder if King Franklin has started brushing up his CV yet.

Probably not because the pompous ass likely doesn't think he can lose. And I bet if he does lose, he'll blame me. I wonder if there'll be a bounty on my head.

The one thing I've not done in the past two weeks is been alone with George.

Yup, avoiding that one like the plague.

Not because I don't want to. Because I don't know if I want to. I mean, first of all, I'm married. Second, he's engaged. Third, I don't know who I am or what I'm doing, so how can he possibly love that?

I don't think he's trying to hurt me consciously, but I think there could be a bit of the forbidden fruit appeal going on right now. I mean, that's what it has to be, right? He can't really have been pining away for me all those years, can he? Because that would be sort of, well, pathetic. Most definitely sad, and it would paint me as the villain. I'm not a villain, am I?

Or maybe I am.

I certainly don't want to be the helpless damsel in distress either though. There's got to be an in between.

I'm trying not to think about George, but I'm also trying not to think about Stephan.

I miss him so much. His smile. His deep, rumbly laugh. His touch. Oh, God, I can't even begin to say how much I miss waking up with his body pressed to mine. I even miss his stinky feet. Obviously, with a man that size and that manly, there are some trade-offs. I don't think I miss his snoring, but on the other hand, I haven't been sleeping that well without it. Maybe I need his snoring, like white noise, to help me through.

He hasn't called. He hasn't come storming in, tossing me over his shoulder, and laying claim to me like a dominant alpha male. He hasn't even sent that security detail he promised. Asshat.

Okay, I've also been reading a lot of romance books. Ma brought me a fresh stack from the library on her last visit. To be perfectly honest, I generally don't like the alpha male. But in this case, some sort of *anything* would be appreciated. Knowing Stephan, when the election's over, I'll probably receive both a warrant for my arrest for treason and divorce papers, all served by the same solicitor.

I don't know what possesses me, but suddenly I need to get out of the house. Long walks through the farmland are no longer cutting it. I want to go into town. Dressed in oversized clothes, with my hair in a messy braid and covered by a hat, I'm sure no one will place me, especially once I've donned my large sunglasses. I just want to be around people. I'm not an introvert. Well, maybe a little. I don't love huge crowds, but I like talking. I feel if I don't start talking soon, I may lose my voice forever. I often find myself talking to that stupid cat like he's a person. Sometimes that's the only time I speak throughout the course of the day.

So I'll head into town. I don't have tons of money, so I'll window shop. You know, like nothing's changed, and I'm still the poor girl who was deserted by her father. Her husband. I mean, I know *technically* I left, but Stephan abandoned me in the name of the country probably before we were even married. If he was ever there for me to begin with. I shake those thoughts from my head and park my car. I use a lot on the edge of the shopping district so I can stroll around and enjoy this beautiful, crisp day.

In case there was any doubt, I am an idiot.

I grew up here. I'm the freakin' princess. I don't know why I thought I'd blend in. Too bad I've already been browsing for at least thirty minutes. People watching. Experiencing sights and sounds that are familiar and new all at the same time. The smell of the bakery. The clanking and buzz from the auto shop. The strobe lights from the variety store. It all had my rapt attention.

Again, I'm an idiot.

It takes a literal flashing light to alert me to the first cell phone camera snapping my image. Then, it's all I can see. They're everywhere.

I am so totally screwed.

In the first place, I'm not supposed to be out in public. This is going to draw questions about what I'm doing here. Then, let's discuss how I look. I don't even want to imagine the tabloid fodder my appearance will inspire. The mere thought of it makes my stomach roll, and I suppress the urge to vomit. There was a reason why I didn't go online much when I had my phone. The press is like, way cruel. They seem to forget that I'm a person and that their words can hurt me.

Yeah, I won't be looking this time.

I can only imagine that King Franklin and Stephan will blow a gasket over this. I need to try to minimize damage. I make a mental note not to say anything against the monarchy, if it comes up. I glance around. No one's approaching me yet, so maybe I'm off the hook there.

Or not.

"Princess Maryn! What a surprise to see you here! Out stumping for the election?"

I don't need a visual confirmation. I'd recognize the voice anywhere. Kamera Simonski. My arch nemesis.

Good God, could my life get any more clichéd?

"Oh, no, I'm just out enjoying the beautiful weather." I paste on my most regal smile. I try to pretend that I don't look like something the cat dragged in.

"Yes, but here? In Benssimon?" Kamera is looking me up and down. I'd like to check her out as well, but I'm trying to hold my head up high. Literally. "Looking so ..." She trails off. She doesn't need to say more. I know where she's going.

Except I don't. Kamera leans in. "I'm sorry about ... you know. That was quite a shock on the telly this morning. But if you're here to hide, you're not successful. I'm sure the whole world knows by now." She nods to another bystander, filming our encounter.

"What exactly are you sorry about?" Damn, I said that wrong. And Kamera's the type to notice, too.

"Oh, our poor Princess." If her voice were any more patronizing, well, I'd probably punch her. Frankly, I'm not ruling out that option just yet. "You saw the news, didn't you? That's why you left the louse and came back home, right?"

I have no idea what she's talking about. "Oh, no, that's not it at all. I just thought I'd have a few days rest and wanted to come back here to do it," I say, in my most convincing tone.

"Really? You're not wearing your ring."

I look down at my empty hand. Leave it to Kamera to notice that.

"Um, yes. I don't wear it outside the palace, unless you know, I have people with me. Security and all. It's quite valuable." So valuable that it's floating around in the bottom of a bag in my room. I don't want anyone to know it's there, lest they try to break into my house.

"Right." She eyes my hand again. "But what about the news? What about this morning? Are you here because of that?"

"Oh, you know how these things are. Nothing of consequence. Nothing that actually matters. We are totally fine and carrying on as if nothing has changed."

Kamera frowns. No, it's not a frown. She wrinkles her nose like something smells horrible. "Right then. I, well, I guess I should be going then." She starts to walk away but turns back. "You know, if you're going to be out in public, you should look in a mirror first. You look awful."

And this is why I hate Kamera. Also because she told everyone I stuffed my bra, and also because she sucked face with George about three seconds after I broke up with him. For the record, there are other reasons, but those two carry the most weight.

This encounter leaves me tired and frazzled. I don't want to be out anymore, but now I'm afraid to go home. What if people follow me back there? I hurry back to my car, weaving in and out of side streets and alleys, hoping I'm sly enough to avoid detection.

Yeah, there's a reason I'm not in charge of my own security detail. Man, if Stephan were here, he'd kill me.

Chapter 19

I don't know what to do. I need help. My first instinct is to call Stephan, but I don't want to do that. He should send some people to help, really. The press is all over my yard, and they're starting to piss me off. I can't even open the door without them yelling and snapping pictures. They're sneaking right up to the windows. I've got all the curtains drawn and shades down, but I'm still fearful they can see in.

This is worse than when we first went public. At least I had Stephan with me then. He'd tuck me into his side, his large frame dwarfing mine, and I'd feel as if nothing would ever be able to hurt me. Ha. What a joke.

Maybe he'd send Daniel or someone to deal with these people and tell them to leave me alone. It's the least he could do for me.

I do find a more secure place for my ring though. I can only imagine the press I'd receive if I lost it. Once it's well hidden in a bottle of vitamins on my dresser, I start to pace. I need to do something. I've been trapped in the house for two days now. I can hear people all night long, and they're not quiet during the day either.

I know I should turn on the TV to see what's being reported, but I can't bring myself to do it.

This is why I'd never be a good queen. I'm not even a good storybook princess. I'm a coward. Running and hiding with my tail between my legs, hoping that my denial of the situation will somehow magically make it all better.

I don't want to be a coward. My mother didn't raise me to be a coward. I'm going to face the mob. But first, I'd better shower and do my hair. Let's face it, the press is all about appearances.

Without Phaedra and Claudine, the process is slow and tedious, and I don't look half as good as I know I can. At least I don't look like a bum anymore. At least I hope not. Dressed in a Michele original, I give myself one last pep talk before opening the door.

Except I can't bring myself to open the door and face the crowd. I'm scared. Another reason I'm not cut out for this life. Maybe I should call George and see if he'll come help me.

Damn it; I can't do that either. I really could use a fairy godmother about now.

Since that's not going to happen, I do need to figure out something. Maybe Dina Marie would come over with her shotgun and be my bodyguard. After she realized who I actually am, we exchanged some awkward chitchat before deciding that we could coexist without difficulty. Apparently the thing that irritated her about me the most was that I caused this influx of people to the property. She's not going to be thrilled, but she may help me get rid of them. That might work. As long as George hasn't told her about the kiss and all that, we still should be okay. I still can't believe he kissed me. I can't believe I'm thinking about it at a moment like this.

Shaking my head to clear my thoughts helps only slightly. I find the phone Ma gave me and call George's. I'll ask whomever answers for help. Put this one in fate's hands.

Dina Marie is the answer to my prayers. Or at least my phone call. A quick explanation of the situation, and she agrees to come over for assistance.

"Thank you so much. I ... I need to talk to the press to get them to leave me alone, but they're scary."

"They won't be so scary when I'm there, fully armed."

"Is that even legal?"

"Honey, if it isn't, I'm pretty sure I've got an in with someone at the palace who can get me a pardon."

It takes a moment after she disconnects for me to realize she means me. I like Dina Marie. I think I could be friends with this blunt, outspoken American. She's different from Michele, but the candidness they have in common is something I both admire and appreciate. But the situation with Dina Marie is bound to become messy. I don't see how she and George will survive, even if I continue to reject his advances. I mean, there's obviously no way he'll still marry her, and she's bound to hate me for it.

That's another problem for another day.

I hear the commotion as Dina Marie approaches the back door. Her voice rises above the paparazzi, and I do hear the word "shoot." A few times.

I rush to the door, undo the locks and latches, and quickly let Dina Marie in.

"Girl, you are in some serious sh—do-do here."

"I know. It's why I called. I'm going to ask them to leave, but I didn't want to be alone when I did it." My voice drops. "They sort of scare me."

"And right they should. I mean, hello? Princess Diana?"

"Well, I'm not going to go zooming through the streets at breakneck speed, but still, there's a lot more of them than of me."

"You've got me now. George is out in the orchard, but I can call him if we need him."

"Um, no! I don't need him. I mean, I hope I won't need him," I cover quickly. I've got too much on my plate right now. I simply cannot deal with him— them—too.

"Okay, well, I told him I was coming over to help. He's on standby."

It's obvious she has no idea about George's feelings. Good. Let's keep it that way. I've too much on my mind to think about that situation anyway, but it's another mess I don't want to face right now. Dina Marie seems to be a good woman. She probably deserves a good man like George.

We all know I certainly don't deserve him.

Of course, that doesn't necessarily mean I don't *want* him. That sudden thought startles me. I absolutely cannot be thinking about that right now. I have to face the firing squad.

"Are we ready?" I look at Dina Marie and smooth down my hair. At least I'm wearing a Michele original. Maybe they won't notice that my hair lacks its usual shine and body and that my makeup isn't as polished and flawless as normal. Dina Marie gives me a curt nod, her grip on her shotgun tightening.

I return her nod and head toward the front door. I feel as if I may vomit. Or pass out. Or both.

No, I will not swoon. I can be strong. I'm running through things in my head. I'm just going to say that I came out here for a bit of a rest, as the palace life is quite busy, and that I'll be returning to the palace shortly. It's going to be fine.

I am so in over my head. Without a doubt, the pictures that are being relentlessly snapped will have me looking like a constipated owl. The questions are firing right and left, and I'm not sure where to start. I look from one side to the other, trying to find ... I don't even know. A friendly face? Someone who looks like they don't want to kill me?

I settle on a bland looking woman right in the front and give her a small nod and smile. She takes the signal and begins.

"Your Highness, can you comment?"

Wow. Could she be any more vague? "Comment on ...?"

She looks at me. It's not necessarily a friendly look. I may have picked the wrong person to start the impromptu press conference.

"The weather appears very temperate for this time of year. I'm looking forward to making an apple pie with some locally grown apples." I give them a wide smile. Probably too wide. I can plug George's farm as well. Maybe help out a little there.

"No, Your Highness. Would you care to comment on your comment?"

I have no idea what she's talking about. "I make a lot of comments. Would you please expand?" I try so very hard to keep my tone light and polite.

She looks down at her notebook. "I believe your comment was, '*You know how these things are. Nothing of consequence. Nothing that actually matters. We are totally fine and carrying on as if nothing has changed.*' How do you defend that statement?"

I open my mouth and close it. That Kamera. As if I didn't already have reason to hate her. She had to run and blab to the nearest reporter. The bland-looking reporter, who is obviously a cleverly disguised shark, doesn't wait for a response before hammering out, "How do you justify saying that a child is quote-nothing of consequence-end quote?"

"A child." My mind is moving faster than my mouth can begin to process. "A child," I repeat. Suddenly the world is moving in slow motion. My eyes blink closed and then open. Nope, they're all still there.

I don't know what to do. I don't know how to say what I want to say without throwing my husband under the bus. I don't know how to save myself. Gosh, if ever I needed one of the scriptwriters from *Made for Me*, it would be right about now. Since one doesn't appear inside a magic pumpkin in front of me, I decide to do what I do best. Be honest.

"Yes, well, I was attempting to walk around without drawing attention, as I'm sure you can tell from the pictures. Obviously, I wasn't camera ready." This draws a small laugh from the reporters. "No offense to you nice people, but we don't follow the news. Not because it's not valuable. It is. I miss knowing what's going on from moment to moment. However, I've put myself on a virtual media ban because, well, some of your colleagues can be, well mean." I know I probably sound like a bumbling idiot, but I keep rolling with it. "It's terribly hard to hear about how awful you look or how much weight you've put on or if your body language indicates your marriage is crumbling. All. The. Time. So, it's better for my sanity if I don't see it all the time."

This gets me a few nods. Okay, maybe I'm not a total mess up. "And so when I was put on the spot and asked what I thought, well, frankly, I had absolutely *no idea* to what she was referring. Mind you, this is an acquaintance I haven't spoken to in about fifteen years, putting me on the spot about something tremendously personal." Some more nods. A feeling of encouragement swells through my body. "Help me out here, before I make any more unforgivable gaffes. Too many more and I believe King Franklin may have me drawn and quartered." The laughter indicates I've won them over. "What news did I miss the other day while I'm here on a brief rest?"

The bland reporter, who now looks a little pissed that I've turned her soundbite around, doesn't answer. The hulking reporter behind her throws me a bone. "The news that there might be a child. A boy."

"Oh, yes. Artem. Well, I admit that was a bit of a surprise to both Stephan and me. However, one look and there's no denying his paternity, right?"

More chuckles and laughs.

"So, maybe not the wedding gift we'd registered for, but a welcome addition nonetheless. Children are always a blessing, and anyone who doesn't look at them that way should be strung up. I should know. My own father did not feel that way about me, and he certainly did not feel that my brother was—is—a blessing. I would never, *ever* be married to a man who felt similarly. I'm sorry that Stephan missed the first fourteen years of Artem's life, but that's not something I can fix. I can only fix my reaction. And I will always welcome Artem with open arms into my family."

Mic-drop. Medrovovich out.

Chapter 20

"What the hell were you thinking?" Stephan's face is so red I think he may burst a blood vessel. He's hulking and skulking around, his large frame taking up most of Ma's small kitchen.

He stormed through the door moments ago, leaving a wake of terrified reporters in his path. I hope they think he's upset about them and not me. The entire time I've been out here, I've been fantasizing about Stephan crashing in, professing his undying love for me. Down on his knees, weeping, prostrate with grief at how I'd left him.

Yeah, that's so not how it happened. He's charging in, yelling. Instead of wanting to rush into his arms, I want to hit him in the head with a frying pan. I mean I want to rush into his arms too but not when he's bellowing like a walrus. This is all so confusing.

A hundred responses run through my head. "I wasn't thinking." "It's not as if I'd kept my feelings about Artem a secret." "I didn't know what else to say." But mostly, what I'm thinking is, "why weren't you here to help?" A simple shrug is how I finally answer.

"You've got to do better than that. Do you know what a colossal mess this is? That *you've* made? I'm not sure we can fix it!" I'm sure Stephan's voice can be heard three counties over.

"The mess that I've made? You cannot be serious. I'm nothing. I have no power. I'm but a pawn for you and your father and the rest of the people who decide everything about my life. If there's a mess to be cleaned up here, it's one of your own making. Leave me out of it."

"You can't be left out of it. You signed on. You're in this."

"No, I'm not." I'm doing my best to keep my voice low and steady, in contrast with his loud boom. Partly because I know it's an effective negotiation technique. But mostly because I know this drives him crazy. It's how I win all the arguments.

"Yes, you are. You stood up in front of God and all our friends and said—"

"Wait a minute. All our friends? Who exactly are 'our friends'? Name one person who is a friend to both yours and mine."

This silences him.

"In fact, name one friend of mine who came to the wedding."

"Uh, um ... Michele!" He yells like the contestant on a game show.

"Wrong. Michele is now my friend, but she was there as staff. I can tell you my friends who were at the wedding. None. No one. You know why? Because I don't have friends. All I have is you. You are my whole life. That's it. But the thing is, you don't see me. You see me as an accessory in your life. *Your* life. Not our life. You don't care about our life. You don't care about me!" My voice is no longer low and steady. I'm out and out yelling.

"Of course I care."

It's the kind of bland, patronizing response that drives me up a wall.

"How do you care? Did you come charging after me when I left? No. You only came out when I messed up your image. Not because you messed up our marriage. It's all about what you want people to see."

"You told me to leave you alone." He sinks into the chair across from me. I can see the fatigue around his eyes. I bet his father has been lighting into him something fierce. "I was respecting your wishes."

"So *now* you start listening to me? Did you really think that I wanted you to let me go?" How can he be so stupid about this?

"But that's what you said." Stephan looks confused. Like he really doesn't see how he's wrong here.

"Stephan, what was I supposed to do? You married me for my uterus and to get back at your father. How am I supposed to take that?"

He looks at his hands. At the gold ring I placed on his finger when I swore to love and honor him until death. I glance down at my own empty finger. Stephan follows my gaze. Damn.

"You're not wearing your ring."

"Let me go get it. I don't want it here. It's too valuable, and I'm afraid something will happen to it. I should have left it in the palace."

"But you took it off." I hear the disbelief in his voice.

"It's not really safe to wear without a security detail."

"Yes, well, we shall remedy that. And who was that *person* with you when you spoke to the press."

"That's Dina Marie. She lives with George. They're engaged." I still have trouble thinking about that.

"George."

"Yes. George."

"George. As in your first love, and the man you gave your ... you know ... to." Stephan looks terribly uncomfortable. Part of me wouldn't be surprised if he called it my maidenhead. And he ended the sentence with a preposition. He must really be upset.

"Yes, George is the first person with whom I had sex." I give myself a mental pat on the back for the correct grammar. But it's not enough. "With whom I *made love.*"

There. That will get him.

The mottling is back across Stephan's face. "I forbid you to have anything to do with him."

Forbid? *Forbid?* I don't think so.

"You can't forbid me to do anything."

"Yes I can. You are my wife!" Stephan's on his feet, his hands slamming onto the table. I swear, if he breaks my mother's table, he is so buying me a new one.

And then I start to laugh. How ridiculous is this? Here I am, worried about forcing him to replace a table. Something that will cost a mere drop in the bucket compared to the vast Salzach family wealth. This illustrates how different we are. The laughing continues. It's beyond my control, and it's certainly not helping Stephan's anger.

"You know what I'm thinking about right now?" I manage to get out.

"No. I have no idea what could possibly be so funny right now."

"I was thinking that if you break Ma's table, you'll have to buy me a new one. Isn't that funny? Because I know I can't afford it, and you'd be responsible. Here you are, calling me your property. Forbidding me to do things. Angry with me because I want you to take responsibility for your own actions and your own flesh and blood."

He doesn't respond, so I take it as an opportunity to continue. "This is why our marriage is over. You're not you. You don't have control over your life. You belong to the country and the people, and you're not available to belong to me. And I'm not willing to belong to the throne. Not me, not my uterus, and not any child I would have."

Stephan's features begin to settle down. "I see."

I still don't think he does. I just stare at him.

"So you don't love me enough to make our marriage work, then." It's not a question from him; merely a statement.

"Stephan, it's not that. My love has nothing to do with it. It's about trust and respect, both of which we're sorely lacking." I take a deep breath. "It's very clear that you have no respect for me. I'm a pawn in your game. In your politics. And because of this lack of respect, I have no trust in you. I don't trust that you will put me first. I don't trust that you will be here for me. I don't trust that you will save me. And I don't trust that you will ever respect me. If I have any of this wrong, please tell me and maybe we stand a chance. If not ..." I shrug.

Stephan closes his eyes. "You're not wrong. You're not first. I don't know how to put you first." At least he has the decency to look anguished while saying this.

His words are a blow, and I feel sick. I will myself not to vomit in front of him.

Without saying anything else, Stephan stands up. He kisses me on the top of my head. "You're not wrong, but it doesn't mean that I don't love you. Because I do. And I always will."

And with that, my husband strides out the door, leaving me for good.

Chapter 21

I can do this. I can be alone. I'm an independent woman. I can do this.

I cannot do this.

I'm a puddle on the floor, yet again. I think I've been here, crying, for the better part of several hours. My face hurts.

And I'm out of groceries. I don't know what I'm going to do. I'm pretty hungry, and it's not as if I'm going to have staff show up and make me something.

I start to think about all the things I'll miss. Having people to do things was certainly a perk. But I keep coming back to the realization that I'm going to miss Stephan most of all. I miss his sweet, sexy smile. The feel and smell of him. How I felt invincible lying in his arms.

Doesn't he miss that too? Doesn't he miss me?

At least he's stationed security around the property so I'm not so scared. I guess that says he's not totally apathetic toward me.

George and Dina Marie are allowed to come and go. Ma and Tomas also have entry privileges, though they've yet to visit. Other than that, I'm isolated.

I'm not sure which is worse. To be here in virtual solitary confinement or to feel so alone in a palace full of people. At least Phaedra and Claudine would talk to me. Let's face it, neither is fantastic. Certainly neither is the fairy tale ending I'd hoped for.

The door opens and then closes. I know I'm safe so I don't bother looking up.

"You need to pull yourself together. This is pitiful." George doesn't bother hiding the disgust in his voice.

I stare at his dusty boots. "Is this how you felt? When I left? When I sent you the invitation? Did you feel like your heart had been ripped out and pulverized?"

"Well, I'll be going now."

My head snaps up so fast that pain shoots down my neck. "You can't be serious!"

"And neither can you. Get over yourself. At least get up off the floor. This is freakin' pitiful."

I can't handle the disdain in his voice. Scrambling to my feet, I attempt to smooth down my hair.

"Yeah, this is not an attractive look for you."

His words wash over me like a bucket of ice water.

"You know George, why don't you just leave?"

"Because I live here. This place is my home."

My hands jut out on my hips. How dare he? "Um, I believe we're standing in my mother's kitchen. There's only one person who doesn't belong here."

"Yeah, you."

I can practically feel my eyes bulging out of my head. My mouth is doing that super attractive opening and closing thing that so very much resembles a largemouth bass. "How can you say that? I thought you were glad I'm here."

"Why? So you can be the same pain-in-the-ass inconvenience you've always been, but to the nth degree? So you can disrupt pretty much everything about my life, both business and personal? So I can be at your beck and call? So you can come here and mess with my head and ruin my relationship?"

"Woah there, buddy. Slow your roll. I didn't do anything about that last one. That's all on you."

He steps back and looks me up and down. "Can you really stand here and tell me you have no unresolved feelings toward me?"

Oh. My. God. This is the *last* thing I need. I don't remember George being such an eejit before. Why is he doing this now?

"I don't know, George. Is that what you want to hear? That I feel like I'm dying because I've lost Stephan. Because I'm not good enough for him. I feel like someone has taken a hook and gutted me from the inside out. But even though I hate myself for how I've treated you, when you're near me, I don't feel quite as bad. That when you're around, I feel at home and comfortable. That I miss you and that I can't stand the idea of you marrying someone else. Is that what you want to hear?"

Instead of answering, George sweeps me into his arms, pulling me tight. His body feels alien against mine, and everything in my head is screaming, "No! No! No!" But I don't trust my judgement. Why should I? It's brought me nothing but heartache and trouble. So I tilt my head back and invite George in.

I once knew his mouth so well. I could anticipate his movements. I taught him how to kiss and he I. But now I don't want George to kiss me.

The realization hits as I push him away. "Don't."

George is panting as if we've been in a lengthy embrace, rather than a few small seconds. "Why not?"

"I can't bear the thought of anyone touching me besides Stephan. I love you George. I always have and I always will. You knew that, even when I didn't. But I'm not in love with you. I love Stephan. And I'd rather be without him than with someone else."

"Good." George steps even further away. I feel so alone. I'd better get used to it.

"What do you mean, 'good'? How is this good?"

"Maybe you finally know what you want. Maybe you'll finally be ready to step up and fight for it."

Though his words should be inspiring, they press down on me with a crush I'm not prepared for. "No."

"No? You can't be serious."

"I'm serious, George. Dead serious. I'm not fighting."

"How can you say that?"

"Because it would be useless. I'm not strong enough. It would be David and Goliath."

"Don't you remember that David won?"

"Okay. Bad analogy. But you don't understand."

He rushes forward and grabs my arms, giving me a shake with each word. "Then make me. What. Do. You. Want?"

"I want Stephan to love me."

George releases me, and it takes everything I have not to fall to the floor. "You're a silly girl. He loves you. Why do you think he went so crazy over all this?" George waves toward the outside. The press is still there, just kept back a few hundred feet by a security team.

"Because I'm a wrinkle in his plans. I ruined things for him with the election. Now he's in a bind."

"Explain this bind to me." George sinks into the chair where Stephan had been earlier today. Was that still today? It seems like a lifetime ago. I return to my appointed seat and quietly fold my hands on the table. My back ramrod straight, I use my most diplomatic tone to tell George the nasty side of the royal family.

"Image is everything. Preservation of the monarchy. King Franklin doesn't care who he stomps over in order to keep things the way they've always been. So when this woman stepped forward with Stephan's son, it was quickly agreed that she would be paid whatever she was demanding, and things would carry on as if he never existed."

George flinches at this. I don't need to explain to him how this hurts me. I continue. "I wanted Stephan to welcome Artem into our lives. To get to know him. To make him a part of our family. But King Franklin forbade it. *Forbade*. Did you know they still forbade stuff in this day and age? Well, King Franklin does, because his head, when it's not up his rear-end, is stuck in the Middle Ages. He didn't care that he had a grandson. All he cared about was that he wasn't legitimate, and that my sole purpose was to produce a legitimate heir, even if I was diluting the bloodline."

"So you knew about the boy?"

"Yes, of course I knew. But I was *forbidden* to say anything about it. Speaking of which, do you know how it became public knowledge?" I knew without him saying it that George closely followed all the royal gossip.

"The woman, Domi—" he stumbles over her name.

"Dominicka," I clarify.

"Yes, Dominicka. She came forward, saying the palace offered her all this money to keep her son hidden."

I jump to my feet. "But she came to us! That witch! She's a horrible person. I cannot believe she's doing this."

"I'm sure she's getting a handsome payout for it, don't you think?"

"We were paying her?"

"Interesting that you still consider yourself a part of that 'we,' but we'll get back to that in a minute. I'm sure whatever the palace offered to pay her, an anti-mon group offered even more. I mean, if nothing else, this is sure to cost King Franklin the election."

"I tried to tell him that if he did the right thing— accepting and welcoming his grandson—it would help the cause, not harm it! Not to mention that he would actually get to know his grandson!" My voice is steadily rising. "But what do I know? You know, he pretty much accused me of being a Republicist? I'd never said anything about anything, and he automatically assumed that I was against him."

"Well, aren't you?"

"No! I mean, maybe a little—okay, a lot—now, but I don't think I was when this all started." I ponder it for a moment. "I think I'm more anti-King Franklin than anti-monarchy. Everything they're saying is true.

He's totally stuck in the old ways and is holding the country back. I don't know that Stephan would be like that. I'd like to think not."

"That's an interesting argument. So do we vote to keep the monarchy for the next hundred years and hope that the next guy in line is better?"

"Isn't that what you do with any election? Except of course in America, where I'm not sure either candidate is an improvement."

No matter what happens here, it cannot possibly equal the fiasco that's going on overseas. I'm once again thankful to the Americans for keeping our drama out of the world press with their constant upstaging. I'm also embarrassed for them a bit as well.

"So look around, Maryn. Is this really what you want? This life? Stranded out here with no opportunities?"

I look around, once again seeing the dilapidated state of the house. I should fix it up. I don't know how I'd afford that, but if I'm going to be staying here, I need to find a way. But the very thought of remaining here makes the walls start to close in. My heart begins to race. I'd be so alone. If only Stephan were here. I'd be able to do it then.

"I'd be fine living here if I were with Stephan. I wouldn't care where we lived. I just want a life with him." My words surprise me as much as they do George.

"You don't care where you are, as long as you're together?" The incredulous tone is fading as he's becoming more direct. "Then you know what you have to do."

I'm not following his train of thought. "I do?"

"Yes, it's as clear as the splotches on your face."

Gee, thanks. "Right." Except I still don't know what he wants me to do. Or thinks I should do.

George stands to leave. I spring from my chair, desperate for the answer. "George, wait! I don't know!" My voice is rising, the desperation evident.

"You don't know what?"

"What am I supposed to do?" I feel a bit like Scarlett O'Hara begging Rhett Butler, "Where am I to go? What am I to do?" If George replies, "My dear, I don't give a damn," I may punch him.

He sighs. "Oh, Maryn. You are a mess. Well, first thing, pull yourself together. Then, if you don't care where you live with Stephan as long as you're together, then go be with him. Go back to your husband."

George's words descend on me like a ray of light shining through the clouds. Yes! Obviously! I will go back to my husband!

Except, of course, I can't.

Chapter 22

"What do you mean you can't? Don't you love him? Don't you want to be with him?"

"Yes, of course."

"THEN GO." George bellows in my face. I am so not in the mood for that.

"Don't yell at me."

"Stop being a stupid idiot, and I'll stop yelling," he yells. I'm not a big fan of this side of George. He always used to be so even-tempered.

"I can't go back to him. He doesn't want me."

"Are you sure? How can you be so sure?"

That's the thing. Despite all the doubt, despite all the horrible revelations, it's still hard for me to believe that Stephan doesn't care about me. I know he does. I feel it in his embrace. The way he holds on to me while he's sleeping. He's got some feelings. I'm sure of it. Almost sure of it. Somewhat sure of it.

"I'm not positive that he does, but I'm not positive that he doesn't."

"I'm glad we cleared that up." George begins steering me upstairs. He walks into the bathroom and turns on the shower. "Are you positive about your feelings for him?"

"Yes." I stand there watching George putter around. He's packing my bags while I do my best impression of a bump on a log. "But what about all the other stuff? What about him using me for a baby and to get back at his father and all that?"

I sink down on the edge of the tub, feeling the steam start to rise from the stream of water on the other side of the curtain. "You know, George, this isn't how it was supposed to be. He's supposed to be the prince, swooping in to save my Cinderella-self."

George is in the next room, doing God-only-knows-what. "Did you just say he's supposed to swoop in and save you? Where did you get that cockamamy idea from?"

"All the fairy tales."

George laughs. "Darlin," he says, mimicking Dina Marie's drawl, "this is the twenty-first century. The only person to save you is you. And have you ever considered that maybe—just maybe—you're the one who's supposed to swoop in and save Stephan?"

The security detail must radio ahead to the palace, because the gates open, and I'm ushered into the garage without question. So much for leading a surprise charge in to save my love. I don't know why I ever thought I could catch them unawares. The palace knows my every move. Even though I couldn't pull off the covert aspect of my return, I'm still doing what I should be doing. George was right. I can't believe it. I don't know how I missed this. Instead of running away and waiting to be rescued, I need to fight my own battles.

I conjure up images of women warriors throughout history. Joan of Arc. Wonder Woman. Marie Curie. Okay, maybe not the last one, but I'm sure she had a bit of fearlessness to her. I can channel that.

And, the innermost recess of my brain counters, if this doesn't work, at least I know I tried. I faced my dragon head on, instead of running away. I'm taking on the evil stepmother—or father-in-law as the case may be—and I'm going to hope that good triumphs.

Upon entering the palace, I'm promptly escorted to my suite of rooms. It's apparent I've no choice in the matter. Especially when the doors close behind me, and I hear the click of a lock. At least it's not a dungeon.

That comforting thought doesn't do much for me though. They locked me in here. They *locked me in here*! How dare they? No one has a right to do that. It's still a free country.

I think.

The walls start to close in around me, despite the spaciousness of the suite. If I don't get out, I may scream. Screaming seems like a good idea. Maybe someone will come to my rescue and let me out of this stupid room.

I try the door. Yup, it is locked. So I do the next best thing to screaming. Pulling. Banging. Rattling. It's loud enough to garner some attention. Good.

But it's not as if I have a plan for when two suited men answer the door. "So yeah. I don't want to be in here anymore. I'd like to go."

"I'm afraid not, Your Highness," says Suit Number One.

"What do you mean, 'I'm afraid not'? Don't you have to take orders from me? I order you to let me out."

I've never given anyone an order in my life. I'm not sure how to even go about doing it. I guess I thought maybe there would be sparkles or a fanfare or automatic bowing or something when I made my first attempt.

"The king has given us instructions. He would like to see you now." Suit Number Two steps aside to let me pass.

"So let me get this straight. You're letting me out of my room, not because I ordered you to, but because King Franklin sent for me?"

Their silence indicates agreement. With both Suits flanking me, we head down one corridor, then another, and still another. I have no idea where I am. The only thing I know is this isn't good.

Everything about the room I'm shown into intimidates me. From the absolute opulence to the massive desk. I don't even know what it's made from. Mahogany probably? Or maybe something mined from a Tibetan quarry and flown on the backs of endangered condors under the second full moon of the third month, or something ridiculous like that. Behind it, in an enormous leather wingback chair, sits my beloved father-in-law. He dismisses Thing One and Thing Two with a curt nod.

Poop.

This is not going to be good.

Stephan's father stares me down. Trying to pretend that it's not because my knees are quaking, I sink into the chair across the expansive desk. I have no doubt this whole scenario is part of some form of interrogation intimidation technique they teach in King Academy, if there is such a thing. Maybe if you grow up at Prince School, you get advanced placement credits that spare you more hours of boring King Academy classes.

"Yes?" I can't take the silence any longer. I'd better hope I'm never captured by the enemy. Although, come to think of it, maybe I have been.

"You're back." His tone leaves nothing to question. He's pissed. I'm his enemy.

"As you well know. And I don't appreciate being locked in my room like a common criminal. What's next, an ankle bracelet? If so, can you at least bedazzle it with some pretty jewels? I want to look my best for the gallows." I use my best haughty tone, lest he know how close I am to wetting myself out of fear.

"You are a criminal."

"How's that?" I lean back and cross my arms, hoping to portray casual indifference. Yes, that is the look I'm going for. I channel Inigo the cat, as he would lounge around my house, paying no attention to the fact that he didn't live there. Be like Inigo. Be like Inigo. You killed my father; prepare to die! Whoops, not that much like Inigo.

"You absconded with a priceless piece of Salzach jewelry. I have every right to press charges."

"I didn't take any of your stupid jewelry. The only thing I took was the clothing designed specifically

180

for me. I left all the jewels here, as I'm sure you know, because they're under lock and key."

He looks pointedly at my left hand, which is still naked. My engagement ring is still safely stored in the vitamin bottle, in my bags, in my room. "And what, pray tell, did you do with the ring? Sell it to finance the Republicist propaganda? Perhaps you are the one motivating Ms. Nochten to come forward at such an inopportune time."

How dare he? He cannot possibly think those things. It takes every single bit of self-restraint I possess, and probably some that I don't, not to jump up and start screaming at these ludicrous statements. Be a cat. Be a cat. I try not to be too obvious as I inhale deeply.

"The ring is in a safe place, still in my possession. *My* being the operative word, as it was given to me."

"Perhaps due to your lack of sophistication and humble upbringing, you are ignorant of how this works, my dear Maryn. If you had been rutting around with one of your country bumpkins, like that George Panagogus, and he'd ever tried to make an honest woman of you, then the ring belongs to you. The ring that you wear belongs to, and will always belong to, the Salzach family. Of which, you are not a part."

His words may as well be a slap across the face. "How dare you say that to me?"

"Is that not the truth? The ring was given to you for ceremonial reasons only. Stephan did not listen to me when I told him you should wear it solely for public appearances and that it should be kept in the vault otherwise."

"Yes. I understand that. Contrary to popular belief, I am not cognitively challenged. I was referring to the whole host of other inappropriate comments you made."

"Tell me what was false, and for that I shall apologize."

His tone. Ugh. I want to slap him. I'm no longer scared; I'm disgusted. And I'm done with this.

"You don't know me. You don't know the first thing about me. I'm sure you think you do. But I know you. I know you'll do anything to stay in power, including using your son and anyone else involved in his life as means to an end. Go ahead. Do it. You will get what's coming to you."

I stand to leave.

"Now you wait a minute. Is that a threat? If you go to the media with this, you're only hurting Stephan. If you love him, as you claim to do, you wouldn't want to hurt him, now would you?"

I hate this man. I truly do. The king's not supposed to be the villain. Stephan and I are supposed to be working together to save the country and help his father succeed.

Except I feel like doing anything but.

But if I go against King Franklin, it will hurt Stephan.

I don't know how I can play by this jerk's rules, but I don't know how I cannot. I might save the man I love, but what will it cost me?

Chapter 23

"Here, take this." I hold out the ring to Stephan.

His shoulders fall. "I see." He makes no move to take the ring from my hand.

"No, you don't see. Your father requested that it be kept in the royal vault." I want to tell Stephan about the conversation and how his father accused me of stealing and selling it off to fund a political scandal. Those words will only hurt my husband, so I keep them inside, letting them churn away in my stomach.

"So what are you saying?" Stephan eyes me warily but closes the distance between us to take the ring.

Why does he have to be so dense about this?

"I don't want to talk about it. When I go out in public—" If I'm ever allowed out in public, I think. "I'll certainly wear it. But for around here, it needs to be kept safe."

Stephan disappears, allowing me to slump down on the bed. I don't want to lie to my husband, not when everything is so tenuous, but I don't want to make more trouble. I know telling him how horrible his father was to me would only put Stephan in the middle again. Frankly, I'm not sure I can withstand the humiliation and degradation of Stephan picking his father and country over me again. Simple solution; I won't make him choose.

A few moments later, Stephan returns. He stretches out beside me, but not touching me. As much as I want him to do nothing but sweep me into his arms and make passionate love with me, there is too much hanging between us.

"So where does this leave us?"

I'm glad he starts with the question. This way, I get to say my piece first. "I've been thinking about this. A lot."

"As have I. Go on."

I stare at the ceiling, entranced by the ornate swirls of the molding and medallion. I swear I find new patterns and images each time I look. Plus, if I'm looking there, I don't have to meet Stephan's gaze, though I'm acutely aware of how intensely he's looking at me. "I was wrong."

I know I should follow that up with "and I'm sorry," but I'm not there yet. I'm willing to do a lot for this man, because I love him, but I need to spare what tiny little bit of dignity I have left.

The best I can hope for is that Stephan accepts my admission and we move forward, never speaking of this difficult time again. My life, however, has not of late been a series of best-case scenarios, obviously.

"Yes, you were wrong to leave. I forgive you."

My jaw clenches involuntarily at this pompous statement. Leave it alone, Maryn. Leave it. I coach myself to no avail. "That's not what I was saying."

"You're saying you were right to leave? That seems unlikely."

Now my fists tighten, as does my stomach, which seems to be in a perpetual state of turmoil these days. Stephan and his father may be detrimental to my health.

"That's not what I'm saying at all. I don't think I was wrong to leave. You left me no choice in the matter."

"How did I do that? One moment you're fighting with my father and the next, you're gone. I don't see what any of it had to do with me. I didn't come up with this plan to force you to have a baby. It wasn't my fault. Therefore, you were wrong to leave me."

"No. Nope. No way, no how." I'm off the bed, waving my hands frantically, trying to stop this runaway train. Stephan sits up and looks at me as if I'm crazy, which he probably thinks I am. I don't know how to explain this to him without starting another brouhaha, or worse yet, hating Stephan when all is said and done. "And I'm not looking for your forgiveness. If anything it should be the other way around."

"I'm at a loss here. I didn't do anything."

"That's exactly it."

Stephan shakes his head. "I feel like we're doing a comedy bit like Abbott and Costello. Would you please explain what you mean?"

If it had been George and me having this discussion, it would have escalated quickly to yelling and one of us—most likely George—storming out. Perhaps that's why Stephan is a better match for me. I need to keep that in my focus. Except for the pesky royalty thing, Stephan *is* perfect for me. I know it. He knows it. We need to not let ourselves get swept up in outside forces over which we've no control.

"What I was referring to when I said 'I was wrong' was the position I put you in, expecting you to choose me over the needs of your country. I know I will always come second. That Montabago will always be your first priority. It's a hard pill to swallow, but if I want us to work and eventually find some sort of happiness, I need to figure out how to be accepting of that fact. I am not sorry I left. I am sorry that you did not stand up for me to your father, but I am not sorry I stood up for myself."

Stephan regards me, obviously mulling over what I just said. I'm surprised I don't smell smoke burning. A minute ticks by, then another. I've now busied myself across the room, straightening out toiletries on my dresser. I'm supposed to have minimal clutter, which requires me to put my things away on a quasi-regular basis. It was a compromise after the first week of marriage when I may or may not have freaked out at the idea of someone touching my skin care products. Frankly, it's kind of laughable considering Phaedra does my makeup any time I appear in public, so she's always handling them. I think what bothered me was the invasion of privacy. Another reminder that I now belong to the public. That's still hard for me to swallow.

When Stephan finally speaks, there's been such a pause that I forgot I was waiting for an answer. "Eventually find some sort of happiness? That would imply that you are not currently happy. Is that correct?"

I cannot believe that's what he homed in on. No denying my statement that I'm not as important to him as the country. No defense over his lack of defense to his father. Just that I'm not happy.

Well, duh.

It's at this point that I may become a *teensy* bit irrational. Okay, I snap. "Does this look like happy, Stephan? What gave it away? The fact that I left and cried for days? The fact that when I did return, your father *locked me in my room* like a common criminal, and then went so far as to accuse me of thievery and running an extortion plot. Then, he essentially called me trash and likened me to a pig rutting around in the dirt. This, however, is only slightly worse than only being allowed to attend very boring state functions with you and your father babysitting me. Other than that, I'm left in these rooms to rot. I'm not allowed to work. I'm not allowed to help the people of Montabago. You yourself are busy day in and day out and never stop to think what I might be doing to fulfill my mind and soul. And then, the cherry on top is that not only do you deny your own flesh and blood, but your father says the only reason I'm here is to produce an heir for you, and you do *nothing* to refute that. So, yes, if that's your definition of happy, then I'm bloody delirious."

"I think you're exaggerating a bit, don't you? It's not as if you're prisoner here. And my father is all bark and no bite. He sometimes speaks too plainly."

So this is where I can either fight my point or let it go. Arguing my side will be like banging my head against a brick wall. It's only going to give me a headache, and it's not going to get anything done.

"Fine. We'll agree to disagree." I didn't say I wouldn't be passive aggressive. "If I'm so incorrect about things, then you'll have no problem with me starting some charitable work. You know, like Kate Middleton. I'm thinking—because I love reading so much—that I'd like to work in children's literacy. Shall we see if Valentia can set something up for this week?"

Stephan looks at me, the panic evident in his eyes. I've got him. He either needs to acquiesce or admit that I'm right about them keeping a tight lid on me. "Perhaps in a few weeks. The election is only six weeks away. Maybe after all the craziness dies down."

I'm hearing wishy-washy words like "perhaps" and "maybe." Those words are not good enough and will not pacify me. "No, Stephan. Because, regardless of the outcome of the election, this is still something I want to do. I'll go and work as the story-hour lady at the library if I have to. But I will do something. I've wasted the first several months of our marriage as it is. I could have been helping and raising money and ..."

"You're helping in your own way."

"I'm doing nothing. *Nothing.* I can't live like this Stephan. I need something to sustain me."

"But won't having—"

I cross the room to him and clap my hand over his mouth before he can say something we'll both regret. Frankly, I didn't know I could move that fast. "Don't. I need this. I need a purpose. I'm finally at a place in my life where I'm not working to make ends meet. I want to do something to give back. Don't you think I should give back?"

Stephan nods, but I still won't remove my hand.

"I get that Montabago needs to come first. I promise you I'll work on that, but you have to promise me too. You have to promise me that I matter on some level. I won't do anything to get in the way of the country, but I need you to support me a bit."

Stephan nods again. He speaks a muffled sentence, but I've no idea what he's trying to say, so I remove my hand.

"Sorry, didn't catch that. Do you mind repeating?"

"You matter to me Maryn. I want you to be happy."

"Then don't just tell me. Show me."

"Do you want me to give up my throne for you?"

I step back, sure he must be joking. I say as much.

"No, my dear. You matter. This separation from you has been agony. If I need to renounce my throne to prove to you how much you matter, I will."

I blink once, then twice. He can't mean what he's saying. Being king is literally in his genes. There's no way he could step down or aside or whatever a crown prince would do.

And I could never ask him to do that.

Like something from an O. Henry story, I hear myself saying, "I'd never ask you to put me above your duties. Please, just make me a close second."

Chapter 24

I've been prepped. And quizzed. And drilled. Frankly, it's like being back in Princess Academy. The test will begin the moment I step out of the car and begin my first charity appearance.

I'm going to be reading to children at the library. I'm in a swingy, mid-length forest-green skirt, paired with a navy- and white-striped oxford-type shirt. Michele sent the outfit for me last week. She'd kept up on her promise to try more green for me. Instructions were included to style with nude patent pumps and understated earrings. Claudine was guided to let my hair fall in loose waves over my shoulder. It's a good thing I've got people to do this. I probably would have tried to channel my inner librarian and pulled my hair into a tight bun, paired with reading glasses.

Stephan and I didn't speak much about our conversation again, but the next day, I began working with Valentia and Daniel on my public image and what platforms I wanted to support. More important, this event will be my first one without Stephan or King Franklin there. I'm sort of glad to be on my own. Stephan's been a bit clingy since I've returned. Once I would have craved the attention. Now the hovering is smothering me. So tomorrow, I'm on my own.

It's just me.

Okay, that's sort of—really—terrifying. I mean, it's not as if I need them to babysit me. I'll be fine. I hope.

And I am fine. I meet dozens of the cutest little kids, all spit shined and cleaned up in their Sunday best. I'm trying to be casual and relaxed, which I think I pull off fairly well.

Until the last moment.

It's not my fault. Not really. Not at all, actually, but I'm not sure how anyone will remember that.

The visit had been divided into three sections. My first group of tots were kids ages four through six. Then I had a group of seven- to ten-year-olds, and finally a group of preteen and teenagers. Obviously, the library is crowded, and I do my best to make eye contact with every single child in there. In addition to being good PR, I really want the kids to love reading as much as I do. It's important.

I'm a little disappointed in the teens, as some appear quite bored. Perhaps this is just how teenagers look, apathetic to the world. I don't remember being that way myself, but perhaps I was moody and surly. There are a few in this group who give off that vibe. It's obvious they're only here because their parents thought it would be a great idea. It's okay. I'll try to reach them when they file through and say hello to me personally. I've been able to shake each child's hand, and many parents took photographs.

Not that it's why I'm doing this, but it will be great publicity. So as the last few teens are shuffling through, I finally see the one boy in the back who kept his head down the whole time. He didn't look up once, his curly titian hair covering his face.

"Hello. Thank you so much for coming. I hope you enjoyed the reading."

The boy grunts an answer. Grunts! Now I'm not one to stand on ceremony or formality, but a little politeness and respect would be appropriate. I mean, I am the princess.

The woman behind him is fumbling with her phone. Oh great. I'm sure this picture will be swell. The princess and the reluctant teen. What's odd is that his mother seems to be taking pictures of me without waiting for her son to look up and pose. He keeps looking at the ground, his head bowed, his hands deep in his pockets. From the little I can see of his face, his forehead is growing red.

Oh gosh, I hope I haven't embarrassed him. His mother seems to be doing a bang-up job.

"Oh for Pete's sake, look up." Her tone reveals definite exasperation. Perhaps he's a difficult child. Perhaps—

He raises his head and I find myself staring into my husband's eyes. Eyes that look a little too big for this child's face. Eyes that express pain and remorse. Eyes that dart over to his mother, snapping picture after picture of me.

Waiting to catch my reaction. Planning, I'm sure, to sell it to the highest bidder.

I've only an instant to figure out my reaction. I do what comes most naturally. Pulling the boy into a tight embrace, I whisper into his ear, "I'm so happy to finally meet you, Artem." This, of course, breaks at least a dozen rules of royal protocol, but I don't care. I know what it's like not to be wanted by your father. This may not help him one iota, but he needs to know that people care.

Stepping back, I take a good look at the boy. He is so handsome. Still a bit in that awkward stage where his hands and feet seem just a bit too big. He's taller than I am, like most people, but he's not as tall as Stephan yet. I bet he's got more growing to do. Still holding onto Artem's hands, I look around for Valentia. One glance at her panic-stricken face tells me that I won't need to be providing introductions.

"Valentia, I'd like to take Artem for ice cream—or coffee." I correct myself quickly. I don't want to be one of those lame adults who treats a teenager like a child. "And have a chat with him. Would you please make arrangements? We can go as soon as we're done here. Artem," I turn to the boy, "is that all right with you?"

He mumbles what I think is a "Sure." His posture has returned to the withdrawn teenager. This is probably going to be an uphill battle to get through to him.

Finally, I allow myself to look at his mother. Emotions fill me, most of them unkind ones. Apparently, I'm not the only one. She's virtually seething. Good. Let her stew. "I'll be taking Artem out for a snack. Does he have a cell phone to contact you as to when he'll be home?"

"If you are taking my child, I will be accompanying him."

Oh no. That will not be acceptable. I want to talk to Artem without *her* there. I want to know what he's been told about his family. Plus, I know she tried to set me up. I didn't have a whole lot of respect for the woman to begin with, and that took the rest of it.

"I'm sure palace-level security should be quite sufficient. If it's enough for Her Highness, it's enough for your son." The voice behind me, Thing One, surprises me. I wasn't thrilled that my security detail for the day included the king's personal henchmen. His defense of me is a new development.

"Artem, would you like to go have a chat? It'll be just us. I mean, they'll be there too," I nod toward the security crew, "but we'll have a chance to talk, the two of us."

"Yes. I mean, yes Your Highness." His voice is more than a mumble, but not by much.

I look at Dominicka Nochten. The look on her face shows her displeasure with this situation. She's obviously pissed I didn't react the way she'd hoped. Surveying her head to toe, I see nothing about her that screams "struggling single mother." Her hair is long and shiny, the black tresses obviously well hydrated and styled. Her makeup and nails are at least as professional as mine. The Louis Vuitton bag on her arm and the tell-tale red soles of her shoes show she is not afraid to spend money on herself.

"I'll make sure Artem gets home safely. Is there a time you would like him home?"

"I don't want him going with you, or even having anything to do with you, in the first place."

"If you didn't want him to have anything to do with me, perhaps you should not have specifically brought him to see me. I'm guessing, from his level of enthusiasm, that this was not his idea of a good time. Since you felt it was so important that he and I meet,

I'd like to spend some quality time getting to know him." I want to add that I'll bet he's got lots to share, but I don't want to anger the bull. Poke and prod a bit, yes. Anger, no.

Artem waits patiently while my security team clears the way for my exit. I make sure to thank the library staff and assure them that I'd love to come back again. It's the truth. Today was fun. I'd happily do it again.

The car ride is awkward, to say the least. I don't know if Artem's usually this sullen or if it's the extreme situation. Either way, he's not much of a conversationalist. The driver, after conferring with Thing One and Thing Two, take us to a small coffee shop with a semi-private back booth. We have to wait in the car while they clear the other patrons out of the shop.

"I felt really weird the first time Stephan—His Royal Highness—and I were going somewhere, and they had to clear it out like this. I wasn't used to anything nice or fancy. It used to make me feel very odd, but I suppose I've now grown accustomed to it."

Artem grunts something that cannot be discerned as affirmative or negative.

I run through multiple things to say in my head and dismiss them all as, well, stupid. Finally, Thing Two opens the door and we're ushered into the coffee shop. Artem shuffles toward the counter, but Thing One steps in front of him and indicates the booth toward the back, away from the windows.

"But I thought we were getting coffee?" It's about the longest and most audible sentence he's said.

"We will." I place a hand on his back and steer him a bit. "We'll tell them," I nod toward the henchmen, "and they'll get it for us. There's, uh, a protocol."

I explain to Artem how someone from the palace has to supervise the making of our beverages, as well as anything we might want to eat, for our protection.

"What if, like, someone in the palace wanted to off you? Couldn't they just slip the poison in or something?"

It's the first real engagement Artem has shown, so I run with it. "I suppose. However, if that were the case, I'd likely be toast already." I lean in a bit closer and whisper, hoping the goons can't hear, "I'm not well liked by King Franklin."

"Really? Why not? You seem cool. I mean, for an old lady. My mom thought you were going to get all flustered and freak out if you even figured out who I was."

"It's, well, as plain as your face who you are. I look at your father every day. I'm surprised more people don't notice it."

"Sometimes they do, and I just ignore it. I mean, it's been part of my life, you know." He shrugs. I don't speak teen, so I don't know. Although, now that I think about it, this is somewhat like having a conversation with Michele. I try to keep up.

"It must have been a shock a few weeks ago, though. Have things been okay since then? Is there anything you need?" I have an overwhelming desire to protect this boy. I get the distinct impression that his mother isn't really looking out for him. Whether I want to admit it or not, Artem's bringing out my maternal side.

"A few weeks ago? No, man. I've known for, like, years. Everybody sort of knows."

"Your father didn't know. Not until about six weeks ago."

There's a pause in the conversation as Thing Two brings our drinks over. I've got a green tea latte, while Artem is drinking a chai. A plate of cookies, fresh from the oven, is also provided.

"No, you've got it wrong. He's known, like, my whole life." Artem speaks with his mouth full, shoving the whole cookie in in one bite.

I take a minute to process what Artem's saying. It can't be true. I was there when Daniel told Stephan. He had no idea who the mother was and truly appeared to have no prior knowledge of the situation. Daniel had been in the dark as well.

"Why do you think Prince Stephan knew about you?"

"Because he's been paying for me my whole life. My mom gets a check from the royal bank every month."

And that's when my world collapses.

Chapter 25

I'm done giving chances. I'm done forgiving wrongs. I am done. So done. And I'm about to lose it. Like seriously lose it.

Except I've got this kid sitting in front of me, so that probably wouldn't be good.

Vomit. Vomit is probably going to happen. Yes, it's definitely going to happen. I rush to my feet. "I'll be right back."

Pushing past Thing One and Thing Two, who are now on high alert that something's not right, I make it into the bathroom before losing the contents of my stomach in the sink.

He knew all along. He's been paying this woman off. He's denied his own son.

He lied to me.

There's no way I can forgive this.

There's also no way I can clean up this mess. A knock on the door startles me. It's one of the Things. "Are you all right in there, Your Highness?"

I'll bet the Hulking Henchmen knew too. You know what? They can clean up this mess in here. I've never pulled the high and mighty princess card before, but I'm going to enjoy the privilege while I still have it.

Which won't be for long.

I wash my face and pull myself together. Pushing open the door, I give Thing One the order, "I was sick in there. You'll need to clean it up. I don't want it left for these nice people."

The massive guard raises an eyebrow.

"You're good at cleaning up everyone's messes, aren't you? I'll bet you were on the phone with Stephan and the king to let them know about this development," I nod toward Artem, "before we even left the library, weren't you?"

He stands there like a piece of granite.

"Clean it up, then we'll be going."

I start to walk past when I feel his hand on my arm. For his baseball-mitt-sized hands, his touch is surprisingly light. "Your Highness?"

I look from the hand to his face and then back to his hand again. "Yes?" I can't believe he's touching me. What if he reaches up and snaps my neck to silence me?

"What you're doing here?" His voice falters a bit. "With the boy?"

Now it's my turn to raise an eyebrow.

"It's a good thing. Someone should have done it a long time ago."

"So, you knew?" Of course he knew. They all knew. I was the only one in the dark.

"Yes. King Franklin has known since the beginning. For a long time, our assignment was to keep this under the rug."

Even though I knew that without being told, the confirmation knocks the wind out of me. I start to feel a bit woozy.

"Your Highness. Your Highness?" Thing One's voice is getting further and further away. And then it's gone and everything is black.

I don't know where I am. Panic fills me, making the blood run cold in my veins. I attempt to sit up, but large hands pin me down. Great. Thing One hovers above me. The realization of where I am and what's just happened fills me.

"Let me up. I'm fine."

"Are you sure, Your Highness?" If I didn't know better, I'd say there was actual concern in his face. I must be mistaken, as it's obvious none of the palace cares about me. I'm a pawn and an inconvenience. Plus, they think I'm an idiot who can be played. They may be right about that one.

"Yes, now let me up. Where's Artem? Is he still here?"

"Yes, Your Highness." Thing One pulls me to my feet. He'd delicately placed me in a chair as I passed out, and he's as gentle getting me upright. "He doesn't know you're ill."

"Of course I'm ill. This whole situation makes me sick. Every single one of you make me sick." I pull my elbow out of his grip and hold my head as high as I can. Truth be told, I could use the support. I really do not feel well.

These people are hazardous to my health.

I need to be done, once and for all. Maybe I'll go to America. Michele is there, so I'll know someone.

Plus, things are so chaotic with their politics that they won't even notice me. I wonder if I can convince Ma and Tomas to come too. That would be perfect. It's what I need. A new beginning. A fresh start that leaves all of this hurt and betrayal behind.

But then I see Artem, still sitting in the booth. I'd expect him to be on his phone, as most kids seem to be physically attached to a screen at all times. Instead, he's reading a book.

I slide back into the seat. "I'm so sorry. I'm not feeling well."

His eyes grow wide. "Do you think you were poisoned?"

Yes, poisoned by the Salzach family. "No, perhaps just a bug." I've got this last chance to get information before I confront Stephan. "So, have you met your father?"

Artem shakes his head. "I want to. My mom says it's not allowed until I'm eighteen. I don't get that. It seems stupid."

"Agreed."

"I mean, why doesn't he want to meet me? Whatever. I'm fine. It's cool. I'm good." He tries to shrug it off, but I see the hurt. I know that hurt. I've felt that hurt.

"I was sixteen when my dad left. He wasn't a good father to begin with, and then he ran off with the next-door neighbor. I have a brother who has special needs, and he wanted nothing to do with him whatsoever. But he didn't want me either. I haven't spoken to him in fifteen years. I wish it didn't still hurt, but it does."

"Yeah, it sucks. Especially because I have to see him all the time. I mean not him, but *him*. He's everywhere."

"I can't imagine that. It's got to be very hard. I can at least pretend my dad doesn't exist."

"Yeah, well." He shrugs again.

"I don't have anything to say in his defense. I really don't. I can only tell you that since I found out about your existence, about six weeks ago, I've been lobbying for you to be brought to the palace. It's been met with strong resistance, and I even left for a while over it. I know it won't mean much, coming from your stepmother—" soon-to-be-ex-step-mother, I clarify in my head, "—but I wanted to meet you, and I wanted you in our lives."

Artem looks down the table.

"I know I've embarrassed you, but I needed you to know that and please remember that in the future. If you ever need me, I'll be here for you."

We don't say much else as we drive to drop Artem off at his home. It's fairly nice digs. Certainly nicer than where I grew up. Fitting for the son of the prince, I guess. And now the designer bag and shoes make sense. To think I'd had some bit of pity for the struggling single mother. Ha!

Dominicka Nochten is better off than my mother.

Bile rises in my throat once again, and if I had anything left in my stomach, I'm sure it would make a return appearance. Instead, I close my eyes, drifting off until Thing Two alerts me we've arrived.

Just as on the day of our wedding, the nervousness and anticipation at seeing Stephan fills me. This time, however, instead of beginning our life together, we'll be ending it.

I cannot believe he lied to me about this.

And here I'd been proud of myself for being so accepting of his long-lost son. Long-lost my behind.

With each moment that goes by, I cannot help but grow more and more angry. I'm quite certain it's frowned upon by my Princess Academy headmistress, and may even be a crime, but I really want to punch Stephan. Hard. In a delicate area.

That would solve the issue of him producing a legitimate heir. He'd have no choice but to accept Artem.

I'm escorted directly to our suites. Of course I am. I'm sure Thing One and Thing Two have done their due diligence and alerted the entire palace staff to the fact that I'm on to them and about to lose it. I turn around quickly to see Thing One closing the doors behind me.

"Going to lock me in again? Like I'm some common criminal?"

He shakes his head. "I can't, Your Highness."

"You can't what?"

He takes a step back, pulling the doors closer together. "I can't say what I want to say. All the things that should have been said a very long time ago."

If I didn't know better, I'd think Thing One was on my side. "Are you on my side?"

"I'm on the side of Montabago." And with that, he closes and locks the doors again.

Chapter 26

Being locked in my room certainly has its advantages. I've got plenty of time to pack my belongings. Not the hasty, throw-it-all-into-a-bag pack job I did before. This time I sort and fold and really evaluate what I'll need. There's a large pile of gowns that I plan on selling for money. I'm sure they'll fetch a little coin. Other than that, it's mostly clothes, toiletries, and books. I mean, what else would I have? It's not as if I brought a sofa or dishes or pots and pans into this marriage. I brought me.

So that's what I leave with.

The books are sorted into piles to donate and keep. The keep pile is still much higher than I would like, but I have a feeling I'll need the comfort of the pages in the coming days. I find the bag with the knitting I did while home. The delicate blanket, so soft and cloud-like, is what does me in.

I know in the back of my head, whether I wanted to admit it or not, I made this blanket for my baby. Stephan's and my baby. The one that will never exist now, because Stephan and I no longer exist.

I'm not sure we ever did.

How could we have been if we were built on lies? I was willing to accept that my husband's wild ways before we met led to the existence of a child. Not ideal, but these things happen. Especially when you're young and privileged and think you're untouchable.

Hours later, I've once again cried off all my makeup and dry heaved several more times. I wonder how long Stephan will run and hide from this. I'll give him until morning. Then, I'm going to the press. The citizens of Montabago need to know who they may be voting for. The election is still four weeks away. But this might just be the nail in the Salzach coffin.

My mind is racing with all the things I'm going to say to Stephan when—if—he returns. I just wish he'd get back already so we can get this finished.

The moment I hear the door jingling, I freeze. All of my well-crafted arguments fly out of my brain like dust in the wind. Stephan is laughing—*laughing*—with one of the henchmen. Then I hear his voice go lower and grow more somber.

"Great. Thanks, Dimitri." At least he's no longer jovial.

Dimitri. I think that's Thing One. I wonder what he's told Stephan. Probably that I'm in a red rage. Which is not untrue. I may have accidentally smashed the crystal tumbler that Stephan likes to use for his nightcap.

Stephan walks in and looks around slowly. This is agony, waiting for him to speak. To know that in moments, it will all be final. I want to fast-forward and get to the end. Not that I want my marriage to end. I don't, but I have no choice.

"I see you've packed."

I sit down on the edge of the bed and fold my hands carefully in my lap. "It's what one does when one is leaving."

Stephan sits in the armchair across the room. He casually crosses his ankle over his knee, as if he doesn't have a care in the world. "I understand you had an eventful day." I want to slap his pretty little face.

"Quite." I don't know why he's dragging this out, but I'm not going to make it easy for him.

"Care to share it with me?"

"Which part? The part where I finally got to go out on my own and be a princess and it was wonderful? The part where your former whore tried to ambush me by bringing your son? Or the part where your son says you've been paying them off since he was born, and that you've always known about his existence? Which part would you like to talk about?"

Stephan's cool facade breaks for only a moment before he pulls it back together. He still says nothing. That seems to be par for the course for him.

"Okay then. Let's talk about the library event. It was so wonderful. The children were absolute darlings. They seemed so excited to hear the stories and were quite well behaved and respectful."

"That's wonderful." His tone tells me it's anything but wonderful.

Damn him. I just want him to react. To do *something*. Be angry. Be righteous. Be *something*.

"And then I found out that you're a lying sack of sod and have been forking over serious wads of cash on a monthly basis for fourteen years to keep the existence of your son a secret. And then lied about it to my face."

The color drains from Stephan's face, which is odd because usually when he's angry he turns beat red. "I don't know what you're talking about."

"Don't lie to me. Have the decency to be honest for once in our relationship."

"I'm not lying."

"Get out. I don't ever want to speak to you again. Leave me alone."

And then he does.

This is a billion times worse than when I left Stephan. He's gone. I've called Thing One—I mean Dimitri—who has loaded my things into a car. They're taking me to Ma's new place. I need someone to comfort me, and I can't go back to George. It's not fair to him or Dina Marie. Plus, I just want my mom.

I barely get through her door before I collapse into her, my face contorting with the tears that are about to break forth. I cannot go through this again. I absolutely cannot do it.

Nothing coherent emanates from my mouth, but it doesn't seem to bother Ma. She holds me and rocks me, not caring that I'm the same size she is. Tomas is overjoyed that I'm home, clapping and dancing around. I look up to see my brother smiling and saying, "Maryn, watch me. Maryn, watch me." He's throwing up a tennis ball and catching it in his hands.

Every so often, he drops it and says, "Oh shucks." At least that's what I think he's saying. Sometimes his articulation isn't the best, and it actually sounds as if he's saying a word that rhymes with "shucks."

That makes me smile. I've missed this. Sure, the last four years have been a whirlwind of romance and very nearly a fairy tale. I should have known that if it seems too good to be true, it probably is.

"Well, Ma, I'm back. For good this time."

"Oh sweetie, I'm so sorry."

I want to be glib and shrug it off with a "what are you going to do?" or the ever-popular "it is what it is" but I can't. All I can do is cry some more. Eventually, even Tomas is trying to comfort me—until he loses interest and goes to watch some TV.

I join him for a while, the mind-numbing preteen sitcom barely registering in my consciousness. Oh God, I'm not sure I can do this either. Sit here and pretend everything's normal.

Desperate for something that will occupy my mind, I start unpacking some of my clothes. I'm fortunate there's a spare bedroom here. I do think we'll return to the old home once everything is finalized. I remain adamant in my decision to demand that Stephan support my mother and brother. I don't want much out of this marriage. Just security. You know, the one thing he didn't provide for me.

Ma leaves me alone, which is probably a good thing. Every time she tries to talk to me, I burst out in tears. I can pull it together and dry up a bit, until I have to speak to her again. Even if it's something as innocuous as asking me what I want to eat. Everything she says seems to trigger me. Good God, this phase cannot end soon enough. And the complete injustice of it all is that Stephan won't shed a tear. Not one single molecule of moisture will leak from his eyes over me. I was under the delusion that at some point in our relationship, I'd break through that wall and expose the emotion underneath. Now I wonder what's even under there. It's certainly not what I thought.

I thought he was a good man.

I thought he had good intentions toward both me and his country.

I thought wrong.

Night falls and I turn on every light in my room to shoo away the dark. I don't care how tired I am, and boy am I exhausted, but I don't want to try to go to sleep. I consider drinking myself into a stupor, but I have a feeling that it won't help. Not to mention the idea of alcohol is repugnant at this point. Reading is useless, and I can't focus enough to knit. I know this because I try to start a scarf, but after ripping out the cast-on stitches for the fifth time, I give up. It's hopeless. I'm hopeless.

I must finally doze off, because I'm startled and confused by a commotion out in the living room. I hear Ma—what time is it anyway?—her voice growing louder. "No, I don't think that's a good idea. She's finally asleep. You don't understand. She's not well."

"I know she's not well. I'm here to fix that."

I hear Tomas's voice. "Ma said no. That means no. You need to listen the first time."

I love the fact that my little brother is trying to defend me. And while I appreciate it, I'm done being the damsel in distress. It's time for me to slay my own dragon.

"Stephan, what do you want? What could you possibly have left to say?"

He rushes toward me. "Maryn, please. You have to listen."

I step back, dodging his embrace. The foot of space between us might as well be a vast chasm. Out of the corner of my eye, I see Ma urge Tomas into his room. I imagine Ma will have her ear pressed to the door. I know I certainly would.

"Why would I listen to you? It's not like I can believe any single word that comes out of your lying mouth."

Stephan's mouth trembles. I wonder if it's because he can't contain all the lies. "Lies," he says, as if reading my thoughts. "It's all been lies."

"Yes. On that we can agree. Now that we've got that cleared up, will you please leave?"

"No, Maryn, it's what I'm trying to tell you. All the lies. They're costing me everything, and they're not even my lies."

The word "lies" has been said entirely too many times, and it's beginning to lose its meaning, like when you say "tree" over and over. For some stupid reason, it pops into my head that this is called semantic satiation. Why am I thinking about this right now? Oh right. All the lies. I can't even begin to respond to him, so he continues talking.

"No, it's not me who lied. It's them."

"Who's them?" If there's one thing that irritates me, it's not accepting responsibility for one's actions. Stephan should know this about me. We've had long talks about it in the past. I guess it's a detail he forgot. Like the existence of his son.

"All of them."

This is infuriating. "All of who?" I can't keep going like this. I'm not pulling teeth to get to the bottom of his cock-and-bull story.

"They knew. All this time. They knew about Artem."

"Don't you mean *we* knew?"

"NO." He's emphatic, grasping tightly onto my arms, which are pinned at my side. This is not the most comfortable position.

"You're squishing me."

More gingerly than I would expect from a man his size, Stephan picks me up and sits down on the couch, carefully cradling me in his arms. Desperation seeps through his touch, so rather than fight to get away, I let him hold me. He buries his head in my neck, and I feel his trembling.

"They've cost me everything. Everything."

"Who? What? I don't know what you're talking about."

"Ever since the day Daniel came in and told us about Artem, I've tried not to let it bother me. And yes, that was the first time I ever heard I had a child. A son. I didn't want to let it get to me. But it did. The first thing I did was go to my father and urge him to bring Artem to the palace. He told me no. And went on, in great detail, as to why it wasn't a good idea. All the reasons I told you."

"But you agreed with your father."

"I had to, but it wasn't how I really felt. I wanted to meet my son. I wanted to be a father. I know this will seem like a difficult concept to understand, but I didn't really have a father."

"Excuse me?"

"He wasn't my father. First and foremost, he was the king. He belonged to the people of Montabago. And to generations of Salzach monarchs before him. But not to the little boy who just wanted to play. I know it's confusing."

"Not really. Not at all."

"Why do you say that?"

"Mostly because that's how our marriage is. Was," I quickly correct. "You are married to Montabago first and me a very distant second. I was trying to come to terms with that, and that's a hard enough pill to swallow, but I can't choke it down when it's all based on lies."

"It is, but it's not me. I'm not the one who lied." His voice is desperate, pleading. "Listen to me, please. I didn't know about Artem, I swear. But *he* did."

There's no need to ask for clarification as to who the *he* is. "What do you mean, he knew?"

"Right from the beginning. Before Artem was even born. Dominicka went to the palace when she was still pregnant. He offered her money right from the beginning to stay away and never tell me."

My heart breaks for Stephan a bit. "Why would he do that? I mean, he's a mean old bastard, so I can see it. But your mom was still alive. Why didn't she stop him?"

He again tucks his head into me, and I can feel him taking deep breaths. "It was her idea."

Queen Margarethe had passed away before Stephan and I met, so I never knew her. But what kind of mother would do that to her child? And grandchild? "I don't understand."

"My parents aren't like yours. Well, not like your mom. Maybe our fathers are similar. They are ruthless and cunning and were not going to let their son's mistake 'ruin everything' for them. My whole life, they've been counting down to this bloody election. I swear, every move in their lives has been calculated with the outcome of the election in mind. That includes me."

"I'm surprised they didn't try for the spare."

"Oh, they did, but my mother's health didn't permit. She was sick for much longer than anyone knew. Obviously, we couldn't let the people know she was struggling. That might damage *the image*."

"I hate the image."

He looks up at me and gives a weak smile. "I hate it too. One of the reasons I fell so helplessly in love with you so quickly is because of your honesty and your candidness. Your willingness to love so fully. You give love away like it's from a bottomless well. You don't ration it out in mere morsels as if there's a limited supply."

His one hand cups my jaw, and he turns my face so I have no choice but to look directly at him. "Maryn, I can't lose you. Not like this. I won't survive if you leave me. This whole situation is horrible enough. I've lost my son. I don't know that I can continue to have a relationship with my father after all of this. I can't lose my wife too." He looks down for a moment. When he resumes his gaze into my eyes, I notice his are glistening. "You are the only one I trust. You are the only one who loves me for me. You are the only one who knows *me*. Please. I can't live without you in my life."

My heart melts, but something in my head is screaming at me to be strong. This time the head wins. "I'm hearing a lot about what I can do for you and why you need me. What about me? What do I get from this? A lifetime of distrust? Of never quite knowing when the other shoe will drop?"

"Maryn, I know you loved me like I love you. I am as broken by the dishonesty as you are. But it wasn't us. *We're* who we've always been. Please let me show you. Let me love you." One tear and then another spill from Stephan's eyes.

"You're crying."

His hand leaves my jaw so he can wipe away the tears. "Perhaps."

"You don't cry. You never even cried when your mother died."

"I didn't love my mother the way I love you."

Tears now breach my own cheeks. "I hope not. That would be icky. This isn't some Greek tragedy."

His smile is watery but warm. "She never touched me the way you have."

"Again, super icky."

Stephan rests his head against my shoulder, his red hair now disheveled and spilling out of its usual coif. I feel his body shake. I don't know if it's with tears or laughter. I tip my head slightly and kiss the top of his head.

"I think this is the first time I've been able to do that."

He looks up at me, his cheeks wet but his smile broad. "So do I have hope that it won't be the last?"

I kiss him long and hard. I've missed his lips on mine, so I take advantage. Claiming them. Claiming him. Letting my mouth tell him that I'm never letting him go again.

Chapter 27

"Crap."

"That language is unbecoming of a princess."

"Are you going to tell the Princess Academy Police? Will I get a demerit?"

Stephan laughs. We're still cuddled on the couch. Ma and Tomas have joined us in the living room, and we're watching TV, just like any regular family. "I won't tell. I promise. But what are you 'crapping' about?"

I elbow him. "Such language for a prince. I was crapping because now I have to pack again. I'm sick of packing. And unpacking. And packing again."

"I'll help. And this is the very last of it. I promise."

I know he's right. "Ma, will you be okay if we leave in a little while?"

She smiles at me. "Maryn, I've been okay my whole life. I think I can manage. After all, it's not as if you did dishes or took out the trash while you were here. You haven't contributed much at all, to be perfectly honest."

"Fine. Be like that. And I was going to ask you and Tomas to visit me more. Maybe look at a palace apartment."

"Oh, I don't think—"

"Can I get a cat?" Tomas pipes in. I'd thought he was engrossed in his show but I guess not. "If we live there, can I get a cat?"

"Yes, Tomas. We will get a cat for you. I sort of liked Inigo."

"I want a yellow cat, and I'll call him Buttercup."

I don't bother correcting about the gender. Knowing Tomas, the next cat will be Buttercup, regardless of gender or color. And that's a beautiful thing about my brother. I need some of that beauty in my life. The messy, not-polished, real beauty that you don't find behind the palace walls. Yes, they will come more often, and yes there will be a cat.

"I guess I'd better get packing then." I move to stand up and as I do, I feel a crack and then tremendous pain in my low back. "Aaaaaahhh!" I can't do anything but collapse backward, the agony shooting from my back down my leg. Tears instantly fill my eyes.

"Darling, what's wrong?"

"I don't know. It hurts," I weep.

My mother rushes over and Stephan is in my face. "Back up. I can't breathe. Let me try again." This time, I manage to get to my feet, but I'm not quite upright, and I can't put full weight on my right leg.

"Darling, I'm taking you to hospital."

Normally I would put up a fuss, but this hurts too much. The last time my back went out, it was nothing like this. I mean, it hurt but nothing in comparison to right now. The palace physician gave me a quick steroid pack, and I was good to go. Now it's a different story. I can't really walk. Each step is more of a limp and lurch than anything else, and I find myself leaning on Stephan more than supporting my body weight on my own. The car ride is horrendous, as I can't really sit square on my bum. Security—Thing One and Thing Two are back on the job—call ahead, and the ambulance bay is cleared out, in waiting for the Princess of Pain.

Stephan sweeps me into his arms and gingerly deposits me on the waiting gurney. I'm curled on my side, willing the tears to stop. If I don't move, the pain is cut back to a dull ache. I tell this to Stephan. "So, if I can stay like this, I should be fine."

"No, my darling. We'll get you fixed up in a jiffy. I'm sure it's nothing." The worry in his voice sends me into an absolute panic.

"Of course it's nothing! It's not something. What sort of something are you thinking? A bad disc? Kidney stones? Cancer? Oh, my God, do you think I have cancer?"

I wish Ma had come with us, because I think she'd be a bit better at calming me down. She had to stay back with Tomas until a respite worker could come. She offered to call someone immediately, but I told her I'd be fine with Stephan and that Tomas needed her more than I did.

I lied.

So, now I'm freaking out that I'm dying. Cancer is eating away at my entire body, and I'll be dead in a month. I wonder what effect that will have on the election? I'm sure King Franklin will find some way to spin it to his advantage.

I'm shown to a private room where the chief of orthopaedics personally comes in to examine me. This is a good sign. Orthopaedics means bones. If they thought it was cancer, they'd send in an oncologist, right?

I'm asked all the usual questions about how this happened and my medical history, which is relatively unremarkable. "I'm very healthy. I mean, I did throw my back out about um, maybe three months ago, but it was nothing like this. And that time, I was trying to move a table. Today, I was simply standing up, and out it went."

Stephan's still got a death grip on my hand, and that's getting a bit uncomfortable. The doctor continues. "We're going to send you off for some radiographs as soon as security clears it, which should only take a few moments. We'll know more after that."

"Will this show if I have cancer?" I can't help but ask. I feel the whoosh of breath that Stephan releases, as if I've punched him in the gut.

"Your Highness, what you have described sounds musculoskeletal in nature, but we'll certainly look for anything suspicious. You don't have a history that would indicate a malignancy, so let's evaluate this route first. Now, is there any chance you could be pregnant?"

"No." I answer quickly. "Well, I don't think so. I mean, I ... probably not."

"In that case, since we'll be taking film from your pelvic region, we'll do a pregnancy test first. We wouldn't want to expose a fetus to all that radiation."

"But I don't think I am."

"What was the date of your last menstrual cycle?"

Aaaaahhh ... I have no idea. I try to think back but honestly can't remember. "I guess you'd better do the test then."

Getting up to give a urine specimen is a bit more challenging than I expected it to be, and I end up in tears over the toilet. I started off laughing at myself as I hobbled to the facilities, but then the pain intensified and the sobs took over. What a dignified princess.

Once back in bed, I'm too consumed with the pain to think about anything else. I ask Stephan, "Do you think they'll give me a shot of something soon? I don't know how much more I can take of this."

He doesn't have a chance to answer before the doctor returns, looking at the tablet in his hands. His stylus swipes and pokes a few things, a frown briefly crossing his forehead. "A slight change in plans. We'll be taking you down to radiology, but you'll be going for an ultrasound."

"Why? Will that give you a better look at my back? Or do you think it's my kidneys?"

"No, Your Highness. It will give us a better look at your baby."

"Baby?" It's a good thing I'm lying down, otherwise I'd probably faint.

"Yes. Congratulations. You're expecting the next Prince or Princess of Montabago."

Chapter 28

Well, this is unexpected. It almost—*almost*—makes me forget the pain for a minute.

"I don't understand." That's Stephan, and if I had to guess, I'd say he's as gobsmacked as I am.

"I don't either. I'm on the pill."

"When you injured your back a few months ago, were you given steroids?" The physician is still tapping away on his tablet.

"Yes, it helped tremendously."

"Yes, well, as you know, steroids can render oral contraceptives ineffective, and you need to use a backup method."

That would have been nice to know.

"We're going to take you to ultrasound in a moment and see if we can tell how far along you are."

"Can you tell the gender?" I don't know if Stephan wants to find out or if we're even allowed. I'm sure there's some sort of royal protocol for all of this. I groan. Ugh. I don't want to have to deal with royal protocol.

"What, darling? Are you all right?"

"No. I mean yes. I mean no." I shake my head. "This is a lot to deal with at the moment."

Stephan steps back, and a slow smile spreads over his face.

"What?" I don't trust that look.

"For once, we've done something that won't disappoint my father."

His father. Ugh again. "Can we not tell him yet?"

A crestfallen look spreads over Stephan's face. "Why?"

"I know you want him to be proud of you, but I don't want our baby—our child—used as a pawn in his political game. There are only a few weeks until the election. Perhaps we can wait until it's over to tell him."

"Yes, I suppose you're right. He would use it. I'm not going to let that happen to you or our baby. We're starting fresh right now."

The attendant comes in, followed closely by our security detail, ready to transport me to ultrasound. "Men," Stephan stands tall to address them. They likewise stand at the ready, waiting for orders. "The details of this hospital stay, including any news that may be revealed, it strictly private. It is not to be shared with anyone, including my father. For all you know, Princess Maryn has a back injury. That's all. Understood?"

They nod. I only hope they are more loyal to Stephan than to King Franklin.

"Thank you. We appreciate your discretion and protection of our privacy during such a delicate time." He turns to address the transport tech. "May we have a moment?"

Once alone, we look at each other, trying to process what's happening.

"So ..." he begins.

"So ..." I start at the same time. Then I laugh. I mean, what's that they say about you make plans and God laughs? He's so laughing right now. "Stephan, we're going to have a baby."

"So the medical tests indicate." His face is doing something weird. I can't tell what it is.

"What's wrong with your face? Are you having a seizure?"

"No, my darling. I'm trying not to smile. It's all I want to do. We're having a baby. We're having a baby!" His voice rises.

"Sssshhh. Lower your voice or every person in the hospital will hear!" I look at him and match his smile. "We're having a baby."

The tech knocks on the door. "Excuse me, Your Highness. I need to take you down now."

Stephan squeezes my hand, and I squeeze back. We're having a baby.

My gurney just reaches the door of the ultrasound room when Thing Two rushes up. He whispers something in Stephan's ear. Whatever it is, I know it's not good as I watch all the color drain from Stephan's face. "My darling, I'll be right back. I ... I'm sorry."

I don't know what this could possibly be about or what could be more important than seeing our child for the first time. I have to remind myself that this is part of the deal, and country matters will always come first.

The ultrasound is a bit more ... ah ... invasive than I was expecting, but I soon forget about my discomfort, seeing the white blob move around on the screen. There's certainly a head and a body and even small little stumpy arms and legs moving about. I swear I saw him ... or her ... wave at me. The tech says it's too early to tell gender, and she places me at about ten weeks. It certainly would line up with the steroid use.

By the way, the physician should have been a little more forthcoming about that possible side effect.

I'm back in the room, clutching the printed out sonogram pictures in my hand. The physician re-enters. "I'm going to send a physiotherapist down to look at your back. I think you may have a sacroiliac problem, which is not uncommon in pregnancy. The physio may be able to correct it right now."

I'm skeptical, but I know that pregnancy changes everything, including what medications I can take. A few minutes go by before a nice woman in scrubs enters. She introduces herself and promptly begins asking loads of questions about my back and my symptoms. She has me lay this way and that, and pokes and prods here and there. Some of it is quite painful, especially when she pushes on the front of my hip bones. She measures my legs and holds my ankle bones. I have no idea what's going on. For all I know, it's some sort of voodoo magic, and soon she's going to wave chicken bones over me.

She lifts my leg this way and has me push that way. She checks the front of my hip bones again and then my ankles. Giving me a hand, she pulls me up to sitting and asks me to stand up. I'm quite skeptical at trying this, but lo and behold, the pain is not there! There's a dull ache in my lower back, but that's about it.

"You're a miracle worker!" I step gingerly, waiting for the pain to return.

She sits me down and explains to me what happened and how I'm at risk for it happening again with the pregnancy hormones. Great. She wants me to wear a belt around my lower back to hold things in place, as well as do some outpatient physio to help strengthen my back.

"Well, you know, it may be difficult to go to a clinic on a regular basis. Security and all. What would you say to coming to the palace a few times a week? We will certainly make it worth your while." In all honesty, I have no idea if this can be done, or is even legal, but it's worth a shot.

The physio is a bit flabbergasted. "I'll talk with my manager."

"Yes, please. I like you very much and would like to keep working with you. I'll talk with the palace physician and have him contact you for a list of what you need."

She leaves and returns a bit later with the belt, which she shows me how to fasten around the top of my hips. It's a bit snug but does make my back feel more secure. I'm now dressed and ready to go. I've got my pelvic belt and pictures of my baby. All I need is my husband.

Who is nowhere to be found.

Okay then. I will not be upset. I will not be upset. I will not be upset.

I'm a little upset.

This is what I need to work on. Sharing my husband. I know if he could be here, he would. Obviously, something more pressing has come up. And

225

no matter how much Stephan loves me, I need to accept that there will always be things more pressing. I mean, he's got a country to run.

I'm following the security down the hall, happy to be walking out, albeit slowly and gingerly, when one touches his earpiece and stops. The other pulls his cell to his ear and listens without saying a word. I see something flicker on his face, but it's gone before I process what it is.

He turns to me. "There's been a change in plans, Your Highness. Please come this way."

"What's going on? Has the news leaked already?" Heads will roll if the media know about my pregnancy before my mother does.

I'm quickly ushered down one hall and then another. Finally, I'm shown into a private room where Stephan sits, his head in his hands.

He looks up. His eyes are red but free of tears. "He's gone."

"What? Who's gone? Who was here?"

I walk across the room and sit down on the couch next to him. "Please tell me. What's wrong?"

"He's gone," Stephan repeats. His face is buried again. "My father. He died." His voice rises at the end, as if it's a question rather than a statement.

"Wait, what? Your father?" My questioning tone now matches his.

"They brought him in. Heart attack. They couldn't get him back. He's gone."

"Oh Stephan." I wish I could offer more than that. My poor husband. While I did not care for my father-in-law, and the feeling was certainly mutual, my heart breaks for Stephan. For that little boy who simply wanted a father.

"I told him. About the baby. I don't think he heard, but maybe somehow, he did. I just—" his voice breaks. "I know we were going to wait to tell him, but I knew he didn't have time to wait. I wanted him to be proud of me. And maybe happy for us."

I wrap my arms around his back and kiss his shoulder. "I know you did. I'm sure he was." I don't think he was at all, but that's because King Franklin was a stodgy old codger who couldn't pull his head out of his bum long enough to see what a treasure Stephan is.

King Franklin.

King Franklin's dead.

Oh my God. Stephan is the king.

And I'm the queen.

And then I pass out. Again.

Chapter 29

Apparently, I have one of those swoony-type pregnancies. Go me. I'm revived with smelling salts. Now I'm totally like one of those heroines in my romance novels. By the way, smelling salts smell terrible. Nothing like salt.

Again with the people around me. "I'm fine. I'm fine. Please give me space. I need some space to breathe."

I look at my husband, who also looks as if he's going to pass out. "I'm so sorry, honey. I ... I got a bit overwhelmed for a moment."

He nods his head. "Yes."

"Stephan, what does this mean?" I don't know why I say that. I know fully well what it means.

"We need to get back to the palace straight away. There's protocol."

"Of course there is."

"It's ... I'm ... God, Maryn, what am I going to do?"

"You're going to be king."

He looks at me. "What if I don't want to be king?"

"What in heaven's name are you talking about? It's not as if you're deciding to drop out of school or something. This is literally what you were born to do. It's not a choice."

"But I'm not ready. I had so much more to learn, and now my father's not here to teach me. I'm not ready."

"Well, that's how I feel about having a baby, but nevertheless here we are. We'll figure it out. We'll get through it together."

He hugs me and his eyes fill again. "How did I ever get so lucky as to have you agree to be my wife? I don't deserve you."

"No, you don't, but that's neither here nor there, now is it?" I wipe his cheeks. "Tears twice in one day? Certainly you've filled your quota for the year on crying, haven't you?"

"For my life, but I have a feeling it may occur at least once more." He reaches over and pats my abdomen.

"Well, today has certainly been a day, hasn't it?"

"One like no other."

As predicted, there was protocol. Oh boy was there protocol. Within moments of Stephan telling me that his father had passed away, phone calls were made. Smoke signals went out. Lights flashed and dimmed. The whole process is well-choreographed and efficient. Stephan and I are whisked out a secret entrance, returning to the palace in absolute silence and secrecy. We re-emerge moments later, dressed in black, as Stephan prepares to make a formal statement. I stole a moment to share the sonogram picture with Stephan. He placed it in his breast pocket, telling me he'd always carry his child in his heart. I knew this was his way of telling me he'd do things differently than his father. It was all we had time for, as there was so much to be done. Baron Von Windringham has alerted the press with a formal statement. Flags are already being lowered and lights are to be dimmed.

Daniel enters our sitting area. "Your Majesty." He nods to Stephan. "Your Majesty," he repeats to me, bowing his head again.

This is the first time we've ever been addressed that way. The first of many new things today.

Stephan accepts Daniel's handshake. "I'm not sure what to say. Congratulations on your promotion somehow doesn't seem right."

"No, I suppose not when the promotion comes as the result of death."

"I'm sorry, Your Majesty. I know that this must be incredibly difficult. Please know that I am at your service, not only as a loyal subject, but a friend as well."

"I know that, brother. I know we must stand on formality, but please don't forget that you are more of a brother to me than a subject."

The two share one of those manly arm-pat hugs.

"What happens now?" I'm very tired and sore. I'd like nothing more than to go to bed, although I know that's not a possibility for many hours to come.

"I will succeed to the throne in a small swearing-in ceremony. Following that, I'll address the people of Montabago for the first time. Then, we prepare for the public viewing, to accept the foreign dignitaries who arrive, and for the funeral, which will be six days from now."

"Six days! I mean, oh, six days." I try to cover my shock. "Why so long?"

"Six days is nothing. I've heard of kings who didn't have their funerals for four months to allow people time to travel back. This, in terms of royal funerals, is relatively fast." Daniel supplies the answer.

"And we are in mourning for a year?" I know I've been told this, but I want confirmation.

Daniel again answers as Stephan sits there, stone-faced and rather zoned out. I think this is all finally hitting him. "Yes. Flags will be at half-mast for the duration. There will be no royal celebrations or parties. We will have the official coronation on the one-year anniversary of King Franklin's death. You and Stephan will wear black until then. Minimal jewelry. You will not wear your official crown until the coronation, but for public events—not that there will be many—you will have a smaller crown to wear."

"I don't have to wear a crown all the time, do I?"

Daniel looks taken aback. "Well, no. I mean, there are some times when it's non-negotiable, but we can discuss the others."

"Okay, and let's get back to this year of mourning thing. We are not allowed to have any celebrations or anything?"

Daniel shakes his head. "No. It's official policy."

"But we're the officials. I mean Stephan is, correct? So if he wanted to end the official mourning period in about six months, he could do that?"

A confused look consumes Daniel's face as he looks from Stephan to me and then back to Stephan. "I suppose, although I don't know why he would want to break royal protocol."

I wait for Stephan to speak, but he looks so out of it at the moment. "Because in six months, we will be in a celebratory mood as we welcome the new prince or princess home."

Now it's Daniel's turn to be quite speechless as he sinks into a chair. "Well, this is ... unexpected news."

Stephan lets out a short, bitter laugh. "You're telling us. Leave it to dear old Dad to upstage this."

"We found out just as King Franklin was being brought into the hospital. Stephan tried to tell him, but we don't know if he heard."

Daniel rubs his hand over his face. "God, so bloody ironic. This was his strategy for winning the election all along, and now we can't even announce it."

I sit up straight. "The election! What will happen with that?"

Stephan sinks deeper into his chair. "It's four weeks away. It will still have to happen, as our constitution runs out and needs to be reinstated. Obviously, the palace will cease all manner of campaigning and let the chips fall where they may."

Now it's Daniel's turn to jump to his feet. "Stephan! You can't say that! What if it means losing the monarchy?"

"I'll always be King of Montabago, even if as a figurehead. I see merit to both ways of doing things, and I'm not so pompous as to think that history alone justifies a system. The Republicists make very good points about the direction the country needs to head to remain competitive on a world stage. Perhaps I could lead her there. All I know is things will be different, regardless of the results of the election. We're taking Montabago into the twenty-first century."

Chapter 30

"Are you ready?" Stephan looks at me expectantly.

I take a deep breath and exhale slowly. I will not vomit. I will not vomit. At least this time it's a nerves thing and not that uncontrollable pregnancy vomiting. "I think so. Is Artem ready?"

Stephan nods toward the door. "He's already out in the hall."

"Okay, then. Let's do this."

Apparently, the anti-mon faction was not so anti-monarchy as they were anti-King Franklin, not that I can blame them. I was pretty anti-King Franklin too. Stephan won the election by a thin margin. I stand up and smooth down the front of my dress. Black of course, with modest three-quarter sleeves and a boat neckline with collar. It's fitted with a peplum, which covers my barely-there bump. Michele was a bit chagrined to find out she'd be using all black for the foreseeable future, but she cheered up considerably to learn I'd need a whole new wardrobe for the spring. She popped off this dress in about a day. She's got a clothing line coming out in the stores, so she's a bit distracted with that. I'm glad this dress arrived in time. I'm running out of black.

"Yes, Your Majesty. I'm ready." I'm glad the press conference will be conducted in the press room at the palace. If we were outside, I'd have to wear a mantilla or hat to cover my head for the mourning period.

"Your Majesty, you look lovely." Stephan takes my hand and squeezes a bit.

"I don't think I'm supposed to, but thank you anyway."

We greet Artem in the hall; he looks so grown up in his black suit and tie. We made a statement to the world by having Artem in the receiving line at King Franklin's viewing. Not a super-fun place for a fourteen-year-old but his rightful place nonetheless.

We walk soberly down the hall. While the solemn walk comes naturally to Stephan, both Artem and I had to practice. I'm glad to know I'm not the only one who needs help picking up this royal thing. Once in the press room, the audience stands and bows their heads collectively as Stephan takes his place at the podium. He's instructed Artem and me to remain standing, me to his right and Artem to his left, but he motions for the rest of the crowd to sit. I can see Dominicka in the back, scowling. I have a feeling her face is permanently fixed that way. Oh well, she had the first fourteen years, Stephan gets the next.

Stephan clears his throat ever so slightly and begins. I know he practiced this speech with Daniel, but he wouldn't let me hear it. "Ladies and gentlemen, citizens of Montabago. It is with humble pride and deepest gratitude that I stand here before you tonight. To be perfectly honest, which I hope always to be with my people, this was not the outcome of the election I had expected. The strongest claim for a parliamentary system was that the monarchy was out of touch with modern times and the current needs of the people. I can say, without a doubt, that under my father, it was true. My father was a complex man whose first and foremost love was this country. Everything else, including family, was a distant second. The monarchy is steeped in tradition. While that can be a lovely thing, it does not always account for flexibility or a change in thinking. I have been brought up my whole life to prepare for this moment. To lead the people of Montabago. To serve the people of Montabago. However, my birthright does not necessarily mean that I am the best qualified to do so. As such, I hereby abdicate the political seat to which my crown entitles me, and turn the government of Montabago over to an elected body, as the constitution dictates. I will continue to serve you as king, in a figurehead role, but not to be the governmental leader. It is the best thing for the country. For as much as I love Montabago, I love my wife more. And I love my children more. The child I already have ..." he reaches back and grasps Artem's hand, "and the child I will have in the future." With that, he places a hand firmly over my abdomen.

A collective gasp rises in the room and flashes explode. The noise level rises, and I'm fairly confident my mouth has dropped open. I can't wait to see that in all the papers tomorrow. I'm sure it's not a flattering look.

I lean in and whisper, careful to say it into his ear and not the microphone, "Stephan, what are you doing?"

"I found a way to have my cake and eat it too. I can still be king in a figurehead role, but not have to actually run the country. I can be your husband and be a father. To both my kids." He's turned away from the press, despite their frantically waving hands. He holds up a hand, indicating he needs a moment. "And this way, I can prove to you how much you matter to me. Our family."

"Are you sure?"

He smiles, and it's the first time I've seen him smile this wide since his father died. "Absolutely. I mean, you'll be a token queen, so you'll have to do tons of charity work and be more of a do-gooder than an actual political leader."

As Stephan turns back to answer the onslaught of questions, I look from him to Artem to my itty-bitty bump, hidden so carefully under my peplum. Holy crap. This is it. My fairy tale. No, it's not one like in all the storybooks. I'm sure our "and they lived happily ever after" will be filled with tears and laughter and fights and lots of hard work. Because that's what marriage is. When you decide that you *each* have the responsibility to save the other. We both get to be the damsel in distress and the white knight charging in. I tap him lightly on the shoulder. There's only one last thing of which I'm unsure. I tap him on the shoulder one last time.

"Do I still get the crown?"

"Absolutely."

The End

Acknowledgments

To my Albany NaNoWriMo Denny's crew: Thank you for the plotting sessions and helping me figure out where this story was going, especially Shannon and Christine.

My beta readers are the best: Aven Ellis and her knowledge of all things royal, Becky Monson, Michele Vagianelis, Laura Chapman, and Whitney Dineen. Thank you for pushing me to make Stephan a little more swoony, right from the begininng.

My editing crew is also the best. Trust me on that. Karen Pirozzi and Marlene Engle, thank you does not seem like enough.

To the Chick Lit ChatHQ and Wenches. You know who you are and what you've done.

My accountability group: Wendy, Becky, and Melissa. I didn't think I could get it done but you all made me do it. I blame you.

To my parents for their unwavering support, and Patrick, Jake, and Sophia. Thanks for putting up with me and writing along side me.

KATHRYN R. BIEL

About the Author

Telling stories of resilient women, Kathryn Biel hails from Upstate New York and is a wife and mother to two wonderful and energetic kids. In between being Chief Home Officer and Director of Child Development of the Biel household, she works as a school-based physical therapist. She attended Boston University and received her Doctorate in Physical Therapy from The Sage Colleges. After years of writing countless letters of medical necessity for wheelchairs, finding increasingly creative ways to encourage the government and insurance companies to fund her clients' needs, and writing entertaining annual Christmas letters, she decided to take a shot at writing the kind of novel that she likes to read. Her musings and rants can be found on her personal blog, Biel Blather. She is the author of *Good Intentions* (2013), *Hold Her Down* (2014), *I'm Still Here* (2014), *Jump, Jive, and Wail* (2015), *Killing Me Softly* (2015), and *Completions and Connections: A New Beginnings Holiday Novella* (2015), *Live for This* (2016), *Made for Me* (2016), *New Attitude* (2017), and *Once in a Lifetime* (2017).

If you've enjoyed this book, please help the author out by leaving a review on Amazon and Goodreads. A few minutes of your time makes a huge difference to an indie author!